THE CURIOUS CURIOSITY

GLENDA BARNETT

This is a work of fiction. Names, characters, businesses, places, events and incidents are either the products of the author's imagination or used in a fictitious manner. Any resemblance to actual persons, living or dead, or actual events is purely coincidental.

Copyright @ 2017 by Glenda Barnett

All rights reserved. This book or any portion thereof may not be reproduced or used in any manner whatsoever without the express written permission of the publisher except for the use of brief quotations in a book review

Sign up to Celia Ladygardens blog to hear about new releases and everyday life in the Ladygarden Household at celialadygarden.com

❦ Created with Vellum

ACKNOWLEDGMENTS

This book is dedicated to Roger, Sally, Cherry, Adam, Sonya, Mylo, Iceni and Livvy. My father and in memory of my amazing mother.

Thank you to my daughter Sally who was brave enough to do the first edit of this book. It cannot have been easy telling your mother where she went wrong and frustrating when she was ignored.

Special thanks to my dear friend Terri who did the boring job of further editing.

Grateful thanks to my son Adam who encouraged my writing, was instrumental in my meeting Celia, designed the brilliant cover and did all the techy stuff that turned my writing into this book.

Thank you to my husband Roger who made endless cups of tea and through necessity as I was writing, discovered a new love of cooking.

Thank you to the rest of my family for believing in me.

Thank you to my dear friend Celia who shared her stories and allowed me to write about them.

PROLOGUE

The young priest wearily approached the taverna. The flickering lamplight, the sound of men's voices tumbling over one another spilled out of the doorway. He warily stepped inside hesitating before making his way towards the bar. It was sometime before he was noticed then a meaty hand pushed him through "There you go little father."

"Evening father, you look in need of sustenance." Angelos the taverna owner said as he poured a jug of wine and slapped it on the bar in front of the priest.

The Priest ordered the dish of the day, lamb kovtos which was in fact the only dish on offer. Picking up his jug of wine he backed away from the bar and took it into a far corner. By the time his dinner arrived which didn't take long, he had finished the jug of wine. The effects on an empty stomach could soon be seen. The poor thirsty fellow had been travelling all day and he didn't refuse when the kindly Angelos quickly furnished him with a second jug.

When he had finished eating in his relatively quiet

little corner and had been fortified by a third jug of wine, he decided to join the other men at the bar. They seemed to be having a jollier time than he was and he was feeling a tad lonely without his fellow brothers. As he reached the group two of the men appeared to have a falling out as there was a shout of "Θα μου κλάσεις τα αρχίδια."(Literal English translation 'You'll fart on my testicles.') The other protagonist returned this insult with one of his own "θα σου χέσω το γάιδαρο." (Literal English Translation: 'I will shit on your donkey.') Luckily for the timid priest (who hadn't had enough wine for bravery even if he could scrape any from the depths of his being) Angelos intervened cuffing them both about the head before slapping down two glasses of ouzo and shouting with laughter us Greeks γίναμε μαλλιά κουβάρια (Literal English translation: we don't just 'get into a fight'...they 'become yarn balls'.

The priest was welcomed into the huddle at the bar with smiles and slaps on the back. He was of slight build due to his poor diet in the monastery. Watery porridge, tatty old misshapen vegetables that couldn't be sold and the odd unwanted sausage of the Abbots hadn't put any fat on his small frame.

One hearty slap from Stavros the butcher with hands the size of Bouzoukis sent him flying. Only for him to be caught by a pair of strong muscular arms. These encircled his waist holding him off the ground in such a way that a ballet dancer would have been impressed with his pointwork. He was trying but found himself unable to speak because his face was buried in the generous marshmallow mounds of a homespun woven tunic. The smell that assailed his olfactory nerve was redolent of a wet sheep's back!

Accompanied by hearty banter and after what seemed to him the hug of ages, he was picked up by two gripping appendages and sat on a bar stool in front of a large glass of ouzo. The Priest had felt it was only polite and besides he needed the fortification provided by the fiery liquid; which reached parts of him that the monastery mead had never done. But then he had only ever sucked out the last remaining drops of the abbots before washing the empties.

His companion, who had lifted him onto the stool raised an ouzo glass filled to the brim and in a gruff voice which sounded as if it hadn't been used in some time and was being tested out said "Ya mas!"

The priest with the unaccustomed alcohol coursing through his veins was considerably the worse for wear but tried to acknowledge this kindly presence. With swimmy eyes he tried to focus as his eyes roamed over the homespun tunic, pulled in at the waist with a piece of thin rope, which also held up some loose trousers, gathered in tight about the ankles with the whole ensemble topped off with a misshapen black felt hat.

"Ya mas kind sir" slurred the priest and downed his ouzo in one fiery gulp.

There was a great roar of laughter and noisy shouting at this from the other drinkers .

Angelos along with the regular group of late-night philosophers was eager to see what would happen next. He offered up the ouzo bottle then refilled the two glasses.

"Ya mas" gruffed the priest's drinking companion and downed the ouzo in one gulp.

The priest with one arm outstretched, hand curled ready to scoop up the ouzo, struggled to keep his eyes on his glass. He could see it but it wouldn't stay still. As soon as he looked away to find his hand he lost the glass and vice versa. He knew it was there because he'd seen it but the tricky manoeuvre of connecting the two seemed impossible. Swivelling his eyes from glass to hand he slowly moved his hand ever closer, then made a grab but his fist closed on nothing. His new drinking companion took pity on him and put the glass in his hand, guiding it gently to his mouth. "Yasma" the priest smiled at his new best buddy and drank it down in one fiery gulp. But for the priest a novice to the drinking world. It was a drink too far.

Angelos shouted through the raucous laughter of the other drinkers " εχουν παραχέσει." (I am sure you are all familiar with the saying but for those ladies and occasional gentleman that aren't, the literal English translation is "They have overshitted it!".)

The priest's new friend picked him up and threw him over a shoulder triumphantly and strode to the door. This proved too much for Stavros the Butcher who laughed so much he fell off his stool. As the floor seemed rather comfortable he decided to stay there and rest his eyes.

Angelos moved quickly from the bar to the door and opened it on the pretence of assistance but in reality to rifle through the priest's pockets. Finding a pair of leather pouches under the priest's garments he used his pocketknife to quickly cut the leather thongs that secured them. Dropping them into the pocket of his apron he made a great show of shaking his bar-rag and shooing the couple out of the door.

The laughter and comments ouzo-ing around the bar were not fit for polite ears but the gist was: 'We know where the priest will be when he wakes up and wouldn't we like to be there to see his face when he notices his new best friend is a woman' and 'We wonder how many escape attempts he will make before he realises that he is stuck on a remote hill- top farm' and 'How fitting her name Adrasteia is (it means inescapable)'.

"Let us hope" said Angelos "he has some pleasant alcohol induced dreams because he will awaken to a completely different world."

This was when the Angelos had the bright idea of taking bets on when, or if the priest made it back to the village.

Whilst all this speculation in the taverna was going on, the donkey plodded slowly on under the moonlit star studded sky. Adrasteia lay on her side, resting her hairy chin in her giant calloused palm and gazed down on her new possession.

The priest was lying on his back protected from the rough wooden planking of the cart by a large sack of flour. Relaxed in his drunken slumber his arms rested by his sides and his habit rucked up was exposing his knobbly knees and barely hairy legs. He probably wouldn't have been so relaxed if he had known that the precious secret cargo he had been entrusted with was no longer concealed about his person.

Once a year Adrasteia would make the journey down the mountain to the village to stock up on provisions. Although mostly self- sufficient on her farm she required a few necessities that she could only find in Pstakis. After loading her cart with her provisions and putting a feed-bag over her donkey's head she would proceed to the taverna for a meal, always hoping for her favourite lamb kovtos. She would get spectacularly drunk, whence the kindly locals would assist her into the cart before some-what heavily slapping the donkey's arse and sending them both back to her remote mountain-top farm. The donkey knew his way home blindfolded but he preferred to keep his eyes open.

On this memorable and life-changing visit, Adrasteia had found something that was possibly even more precious than her donkey. The little priest was all that her womanly heart desired and she would devote her life to making them both happy.

One could quite easily understand how the priest's mistake had occurred. But if he had been in a fit state to look a little closer at the homespun tunic, he would have seen the little groups of tiny pink-white flowers, blossom of the Wild Almond tree embroidered along the hem. Poppy Anemones in shades of pinks, reds, yellows and blues, around the neckline and sleeve edges. Admittedly Adrasteia wore a man's style of dress and there was a little more of her than the average Pstakis women. Her hair wasn't exactly flattering either as it was chopped on a regular basis with the bone-handled hunting knife that had belonged to her father before her. Wearing trousers under her tunic was very unusual for Greek women but this was purely for functionality for her work on the farm.

However underneath the masculine style clothing there beat the heart of a feminine woman who spent many hours straining her eyes in weak candlelight embroidering exquisite flowers on her clothes.

Little did she know what a trailblazer she was and that in the 20th century woman all over the world would be doing exactly the same thing; casting off their restrictive clothing, wearing trousers and customizing their outfits.

Now alone on the farm after the death of her parents there had been a void that needed filling. A well of love that she wanted to bucket up and pour over a living breathing person; besides that she could do with some help on the farm.

In her mind the priest had been sent as a present from God. She had been a dutiful daughter staying on the farm and looking after her parents until their death. When they were gone although she had struggled she had managed to keep the farm going. Every night without fail, however tired she had felt she had prayed for a husband and now she had one.

Now she would pray that many children would follow, they would grow big and strong like her. They would look after her and the priest in their old age just as she had looked after her own parents.

She knew that the priest would be a bit confused possibly even scared when he awoke from his drunken stupor but she would prepare him a tea of Melisophyllon and Phu and spoon it into his dear little mouth. She would continue to serve him this tea until she was sure that any anxieties were allayed and he was calm.

She knew that he could not help but be impressed with her farm; set on it's beautiful hillside and with a distant view of the sea. The delicious scent from the almond and lemon trees, the sage and the thyme would also soothe his nervousness. In her heart she knew that the little priest would come to love her as much as she already loved him.

And the donkey.

Whose name was Adrian.

The next morning the taverna owner Angelos waited until his wife had gone off to the bakers where she would meet her friends for gossip and bread. This gave him a little time on his own and he was very keen to see what was in the leather pouches he had relieved the priest of.

Opening the trapdoor to the cellar he stepped down into the gloom having lit the small stump of a candle to guide him. Sliding his hand behind one of the old barrels his fingers felt for the small space between the wood and the wall. There was a moment's panic as his groping fingers encountered nothing but an empty space before he realised he must have been drunker than he'd thought last night and tried the next one.

Scrabbling behind the next barrel his finger-tips touched smooth leather. Grasping a piece he pulled out both pouches and sat on the bottom of the cellar steps setting his stumpy candle down next to him.

Looking down at the two plain but beautifully made pouches he realised that these were expensive items and that someone very important must have had them made. Spreading out his cloth apron over his lap he picked up the first pouch and shook out the contents. A second smaller bag of soft calfskin fell onto his lap with a chink. With his heart hammering in his chest at the possibility of hidden riches, he opened the bag and poured the money out onto his apron, disappointed to find enough to make it worth stealing but not the riches he'd thought.

The second bag didn't clink but it was slightly bulkier. Gently he pulled open the pouch to reveal inside a small calfskin parcel, very carefully he put his hand inside the leather pouch and pulled it out. Laying it on his lap he didn't know why but he felt very nervous as to what this parcel might contain. Remembering it had been carried secretly by a priest.

Tentatively he took a flap of the calfskin between his thumb and index finger and slowly started to unroll it. Once he had unrolled the length he had a better idea of the shape it concealed, it appeared to be cylindrical.

Unfolding the last two flaps of leather he found another parcel this time of red silk. Sweat started on his brow as his thoughts started to link together. Priest, on a journey, pouch of money, important package, red fabric. He may only be a country taverna owner but Angelos recognised the traditional colours of the Catholic church.

It took another three days before he plucked up the courage to look at the parcel again. Sat once more on the bottom step of the cellar, gazing down on the red fabric, he gently pulled open the material. Nestling in the rich fabric was a small gold cylindrical container decorated with gold filigree and wrapped around it a piece of paper.

The paper was dated the 'The Year of Our Lord 1899' and contained instructions to take the Holy relic to the Vatican in Rome and place it only in the hands of His Holiness the Pope. It also stated that a vow of silence had been imposed over the sacred relic and any person speaking of it or revealing its presence would be excommunicated from the Holy Catholic Church and punished. A small piece of fragile parchment floated down onto his lap but although he tried his best he was unable to read it so he tucked it back inside the paper.

Angelos had never been so relieved to squat over the hole and evacuate his bowels.

Later that night after ensuring the usual drunkards were past all remembering, Angelos called his three closest friends to a quiet end of the bar. The situation was so serious and the burden so heavy he needed their help as to what to do next. After downing another ouzo he slammed down his glass and looked his friends in the eye one by one before telling them about his discovery. There was a lot of cursing mutterings and crossing of chests and the discussion which followed required an enormous amount of ouzo. But the unanimous decision taken was that Angelos should keep the relic safe somewhere in the tavern and that nobody but he would know where it would be hidden.

The money would be shared out amongst the four of them and if anyone should enquire after the priest, they would declare that he had escaped from Adrasteia's cart and travelled North heading for the city. Once the decision was made they stood, spat into their gnarly hands and placed them one on top of each other. Then swore an oath that not one of them would ever speak of this matter again.

Over the next few days whilst his wife was at the bakers, Angelos carved out a special niche in the cellar wall behind the wooden barrels. Once he had placed the leather pouch in the niche he knocked in a piece of wood that he had cut to fit, firmly in place. The secret and the Taverna were handed down together through the family, generation after generation.

Chapter 1 Celia's Broken Night

Celia knew something was wrong the minute she woke up but had no idea what it was or what had woken her. Straining her ears, she could hear nothing, apart from the night sounds in the garden, the watering- can rocking in the night wind and the fridge-freezer in the kitchen making noises as if something inside was banging its way out, oh the joys of auto-frost.

As she was now awake the inevitable happened; she needed a wee. Pulling back the duvet she swung her legs over the side of the bed and waited for her body to catch up with her intentions.

She smiled at the slight snore and sight of hirsute Roley cuddled up inside his bed with his blanket tucked in over him. This was suddenly drowned out by Ronald snoring louder than a lambretta. How on earth could she hear what had woken her up now?

She'd always fancied a Lambretta she thought as she jabbed a digit crossly into Ronald's shoulder, they were so dashing. She could see herself zipping along the country lanes, hair flying in the wind; except the 'Elf and Safety' police have put the kibosh on that by making you wear a crash-hat and she wasn't risking *that* look at her age.

Celia pulled on her woolly sheepskin boot-like slippers. These are definitely too warm for the summer she thought as she shuffled out of the bedroom and into the bathroom. She automatically pulled on the light switch before lifting the lid and sitting down. She heard a sound again through the open bathroom window, there was definitely something out there. Rising as fast as her knees would allow she pushed down the automatic soft-closing toilet lid but stopped herself from flushing, ran her fingers under the tap and turned the light out.

Once her eyes had adjusted to the darkness, she made her way to the back door but hesitated as she remembered how noisy it was when you pulled the handle down. She must remind Ronald to get the WD40 out in the morning. Wonderful stuff. Ronald keeps trying to persuade her to put it on her arthritis, he reckons it will help.

She shuffled on to the sitting room and quietly as she could, opened the french doors and stepped down onto the patio. She felt the cool night air on her bare skin, naked, she was glad that they didn't have any neighbours. She looked up at the skyful of stars scattered from horizon to horizon, it was breathtaking. In a couple of week's time and if the weather stayed clear, she knew they would be in for a spectacular display from the Perseid meteor shower but tonight it was a black moon and it was very dark in the garden.

St Urith With Well was night-quiet as usual, even in the day it was a quiet. But it was a farming village and there was the occasional noise of tractors and farm machinery working in the fields. She hoped those sounds would always be there as well as the farm animals, the wildlife and the birds. She loved the peee-ay call of the buzzards that sounds like a cat's meow, as they circle high in the summer sky.

At the end of last summer she had been treated to the sight of a sociable group of Goldfinches feather-dressed in bold colours. They were singing their 'switt-witt-witt-witt' song as they feasted on the seeds of a large thistle bush in the field just outside of her window.

Stepping down from the patio into the night garden she unfortunately put her foot down on Roley's red, hard plastic treat ball which skittered across the terracotta slabs. It only stopped when it hit a china pot with a kerching! Bugger she thought as her arms windmilled around and she struggled to stay upright. Balance was not Celia's strong point, she could fall over for a pastime.

She wasn't nervous about being out in the dark on her own, she'd always felt safe living in the village but she wasn't stupid enough to think that nasty things could never happen here. She thought the noise came from the churchyard at the bottom of the garden, she started to walk towards it down the path. Fish! These slippers aren't meant for outdoors she thought as a particularly sharp stone made itself felt but what do you expect for £11.99 bought online on the wonder-web.

1
INCOMERS

The protagonists were crouched behind the churchyard wall. One had a work-worn leather gloved hand pressed firmly over the mouth and nose of the other, their free arm was pulled tightly around the other's neck. The second person had their elbow poised to ram into the first persons diaphragm and a leg hooked around a leg. When they heard a noise coming from over the wall, they had both stopped mid-fight. They stayed frozen to the spot neither of them wanting to be discovered as they heard someone shuffling towards them from over the wall.

Taking advantage of the moment, with a vicious twist and a snap the first assailant broke the other's neck, then gently and quietly lowered the body down onto the ground next to the churchyard wall. Weighing up the options, the killer needed to remove the threat of whoever was approaching from the other side of the wall. I can't be discovered now the killer thought, it would destroy everything and my plan will have been for nothing. If I have to kill again I will, unfortunate as it would be, an unnecessary death could cause complications. The killer crouched ready and waiting for someone to appear over the wall.

2

CELIA IN THE DARK

Celia walked further down the path towards the churchyard wall breathing in the night-time air. She stopped as an unfamiliar whiff of cigar smoke crept up her nostrils. That's strange she thought, she was far more used to the more natural smells wafting over from the bullocks in the field next to the house.

It had never bothered her living next to the cemetery but tonight as she slowly crept down the path towards the churchyard wall, it had taken on a spooky almost threatening air and she felt uneasy for some reason. She mentally shook herself, it was common for her to be out in the middle of the night as she often had to let hirsute Roley out for a pee. She usually enjoyed those few quiet minutes in the dark but not tonight. Girding her loins she started moving again.

As if she had telepathically called Hirsute Roley, he suddenly started barking and ran out into the garden to join her. Not wanting to wake the neighbours, she quietened him down and after he had done a quick wee on the lawn, shepherded him back into the house. The noise had probably been a fox anyway.

Glad to be indoors, she locked the french windows and made her way back to bed. Hirsute Roley had already snuggled back down on top of the duvet on her side of the bed by the time she reached the bedroom. She carefully lifted him and placed him against Ronald's back before climbing in herself.

Always a poor sleeper, getting back to sleep was a nightmare so she started counting down from ten on an out-breath. This technique was the one and only thing she had learned from an uncomfortable meditation class she had attended at the village hall. It had been conducted by a rather loud man (considering he was teaching relaxation techniques) with his grey hair tied together in a ponytail and his own organically knitted mat.

Her mind wandered to a new knitting pattern she was working on. A wrist warmer with the cuff knitted in a warm, soft chunky Alpaca and the flared top knitted in Mulberry silk with beads threaded through. She was trying to work it out in her head when the next thing she knew Ronald was placing a mug of tea on her bedside table.

The crumpled body yet to be discovered lay against the churchyard wall, not much more than forty feet from where Celia sipped her tea.

3

SUNDAY MORNING

Celia took a quick shower not bothering to wash her hair, deciding that it would do for a couple more days then dressed in her 'at home' clothes. After pulling on her knickers she put on a well-washed bra without wires, she didn't have a bosom that fitted with wires. Then a pair of black harem trousers with a comfy elasticated waist. As she pulled them on she thought, why are they called pairs of trousers? They are only one item of clothing even if they do have two leg-holes. Seems odd. She added a vest from Primark and a purple T-shirt bought from the charity shop for a £1.

If only she had known what the day was to bring she would have made more of an effort. Sod's law predicted that whenever she was slopping around at home without a bra and no make-up, someone would inevitably ring the doorbell! Now she *always* wore a bra when gardening after almost clipping off a nipple whilst pruning a Tree-Lupin!

While she waited for her porridge, real scottish oats with half a cup of hot water and one cup of full cream milk in the microwave for 3 minutes 30 seconds, she mused over what she would do in the garden. Surprisingly Ronald hadn't asked his usual question of what's the plan for the day but it was bound to come. She stirred half a spoonful of local honey into the porridge; she had read somewhere about a study of University students, where one half were given honey every day with their breakfast and the other half weren't. To her surprise the honey group performed better in exams and achieved higher grades, that was enough for Celia, it was honey on her porridge from then on. She was keen to keep the little grey cells working as Poirot would say.

Whilst her porridge was cooling, Celia bent down and picked up hirsute Roley's food dish, adding a few biscuits and some meat.

"What's the plan for the day then" asked Ronald as he wandered around shaving, no doubt shedding minute hairs far and wide across the kitchen.

Celia tried not to think about them floating down onto her porridge like dust motes with boots on. Putting hirsute Roley's breakfast down, she moved her porridge out of contaminations way and sat down at the breakfast bar to eat. Scraping up the last spoonful, she bookmarked the page of her murder mystery book and closed the Ipad. She loved a good murder, only in books of course.

Celia put her bowl and spoon into the dishwasher then opened the airing cupboard door, taking out her make-up mirror. Placing it on the draining board to make the most of the light from the kitchen window, she put her glasses on, spun it to the magnifying side and peered into it.

Spotting a gin-spot on the side of her nose and a small stubby hair on her top lip Celia swore. Bugger she thought, why is it when you get older the hair on your head gets thinner but the hair that you don't want, grows where you don't want it to, as thick as a bean-stalk! After a few unsuccessful attempts at plucking it Celia tossed the tweezers back into her make-up bag, squeezed the spot and smoothed on a little 'BB' cream. Drawing in her eyebrows (a necessity after the overplucking of the 70's) and she was ready for the day.

Making herself another cup of tea she wandered out into the garden to another lovely warm summer morning. Her thoughts turned to last night, her disturbed sleep and what might have caused her feeling of uneasiness when she had ventured into the garden.

Sitting in her garden chair, sipping her tea looking out over the beautiful North Devon Countryside. Celia was miles away thinking how lucky she was to live in such a beautiful place when Hirsute Roley came bounding up, turned his hairy little head to catch the scents carried on the breeze then bounded down the garden and jumped up at the churchyard wall that bordered the garden. Stretching his little hairy head and paws as far as he could but he was far too short to see over the top, he started barking excitedly.

"Is it those cats teasing you again poor sweetie? Come on let's go and get your ball." Celia walked back to the house with hirsute Roley unable to resist a treat-filled ball trotting at her heels.

On the other side of the churchyard wall, the flies were gathering.

4

RONALD AND CELIA

Ronald and Celia had lived in the village of St Urith With Well for about thirty years. Unfortunately for Ronald who was a neat freak, Celia was a lady who left a lot of debris in her wake, like a package cruise ship. Things would settle around her like snowflakes, tissues, books, glasses, bits of wool, knitting, scraps of material, magazines, cardigans and her Kindle.

Unfortunately for Celia he was always tidying up after her. And to her annoyance a lot of things were tidied in the bin!

Ronald would sigh as he tried to stuff the overflowing bits and pieces back into her sewing basket. Or when he had to crawl on his tummy S.A.S style to rescue a knitting needle that had slipped down between the seats of the sofa.

Celia was very active in village life; Ronald wasn't very active full stop. Now that he had retired, walking hirsute Roley was usually as much activity as he wanted to do after working all his life. Sometimes Celia was cracking the whip and he was forced to fix something or move a heavy pot in the garden.

Although to be fair he did cut the lawns, put the bins out, vacuumed, washed the windows, painted and decorated and one or two other little jobs but he never cleaned the toilet!

Recently he'd taken an interest in cooking; which was surprising as he had never really cooked much during their marriage, apart from burning a few fishfingers for the children when they were young. He had never been a great fan of eating being an eat to live person but now that he was retired he'd been inspired. He had discovered the joys of food now he was relaxed and had time to savour it unlike arriving home after a long day too tired to be bothered with eating.

His wonderful mother had been a marvellous cook and she'd sent him off to school every morning with a full English breakfast in his tummy and he'd never had a problem with his weight or his cholesterol, which annoyed Celia no end. Well not that she wanted him to be fat with high cholesterol but the fact that it didn't matter what he ate he didn't put any weight on seemed unfair. Isn't that often the case the skinniest women seemed to eat everything whereas she, as the saying goes only had to look at a cream cake.

Celia having a lot to live up to against her mother-in-law's cooking, didn't try. Now that their children had flown the nest and she was able to indulge herself going out and about whenever she wanted, meeting friends for coffee or lunch; Ronald had had to master the art of basic cooking or starve.

Recipe books started appearing around the house with little paper markers in them. Eventually Ronald plunged in and spent a fortune on ingredients and hours in the kitchen preparing meals; believing himself the next Gordon Ramsey, without the language and the blonde hair and the abs.

It wasn't a constant round of gourmet dinners but being a slow cooker himself, he bought a proper one and this opened up a whole new world. As a birthday present he was given a 'Slow Cooker' recipe book and before long he had lots of favourite recipes, producing delights such as Sausage Casserole, beef casserole and Celia's favourite Vegetable Ratatouille with Ricotta Dumplings.

Celia now had the odd break from cooking and it guaranteed he didn't starve when she wasn't there. He had even started to cook the Sunday roast occasionally with a little help but not today, today Celia was cooking. Unfortunately, though they both didn't know it yet, if Ronald wanted his dinner he was going to have to cook it himself.

5

APPLE COTTAGE

On the fateful Sunday of the Colonel's demise, he and Mrs Cottle had attended morning service at the village church as usual but she had stayed behind to assist with the teas and enjoy a cup herself whilst the Colonel went home to mow the lawns.

At home the Colonel was whistling the tune of Elgar's 'Nimrod' whilst marching up and down cutting the lawn in regimental stripes. This was a task he enjoyed and in which he took great pride. He was convinced he had the best lawn in the village. Emptying the cuttings carefully into a garden waste bag ready to take to the recycling centre, he didn't hear anything over his whistling and the mower engine idling. He didn't see the shadow creeping up behind him.

The killer stepped back to admire the scene. The Colonel lay in the bath with the lawnmower blades resting heavily on his chest, his hand clutching a cleaning cloth. The water lapped gently around his body. The lead from the lawnmower stretched across the room, around the door frame and stopped at the wall socket. It was plugged in and waiting for the killer's gloved finger to flick the switch. Watching in the doorway, the killer waited for the Colonel to regain consciousness.

When the Colonel first opened his eyes, he was confused. The last thing he remembered was mowing the lawn. He couldn't imagine where he was! Tucking his chin under he looked down and saw that he still had all his clothes on and was overwhelmed to see a lawnmower sitting firmly on his chest. As his puzzled brain tried to figure out what was going on the sensation of wetness filtered through and he realised he was in the bath. It was at that point, as he looked across the bath top that his eyes connected with the eyes of the killer. The fear hit him, deep gut-wrenching fear but before he could gather himself for flight the killer moved swiftly, flicking the switch.

6
LATER THAT MORNING

Mrs Cottle arrived at the rear gate of Apple cottage and noticed that the back lawn was completely mown except for one last stripe which was unfinished. She looked around the garden but there was no sign of the Colonel. Knowing what a creature of habit and discipline he was, she found this rather strange. So after dropping the bag with the remaining milk and half a victoria sponge that had been left over from church outside the back door, she went in search of him.

First she looked in his shed. He wasn't there but he had obviously been searching for something because the usually neat and ordered jam jars with their detailed labels were all over the floor. Some of the tops were off and the contents, nails, screws, bits and bobs were scattered everywhere. She had never known him not put his things away, not ever; what on earth could he have been looking for?

She was now really worried because if he was looking for something, would he find her secret hiding place? She didn't think she had left anything incriminating where he could find it, but? She hurried indoors but complete silence filled her ears as she stopped and stood on the polished parquet floor in the hall listening. Nervous, she walked to the sitting room and pushed open the half-opened door.

The room was full of knick-knacks some passed down in the family others collected by the Colonel on his travels. Everything appeared to be there but as she looked again, somehow not quite right. Things were slightly out of place, her knitting bag had been tipped upside down; the glass door of the cabinet was open and swinging ever so slightly in the breeze. Oh God perhaps they'd been burgled and the Colonel had been attacked, or he might have had a stroke. She looked behind every chair and the sofa just in case.

She thought she heard a noise coming from the kitchen; she rushed out calling "James is that you?" only to find the kitchen door banging in the breeze. She must have left it open when she came in. This was one of those times when she wished they had a dog. She'd always wanted one especially with the Colonel away a lot of the time but the Colonel had said it wasn't a good idea. Now she could do with it's comforting presence.

Although weak with fear she knew she had to check the rest of the house, she walked quietly out of the kitchen and into the dining room but it looked as if everything was as she had left it in here. Walking back into the hall and looking up she paused before she made herself climb the stairs her heart was pounding. She knew something was wrong, felt it in her being.

Turning at the dog-leg half-way up the stairs and looking up to the landing she saw an electric cable

The Curious Curiosity

plugged into the socket and disappearing through the bathroom door. Now terrified of what she would find she forced herself to move but dreaded what she might find if she carried on up. At the top she took a deep breath turned and went into the bathroom.

At first her brain couldn't make sense of what her eyes were seeing but when the realisation hit she screwed her eyes tight to shut out the sight, but it didn't stop her seeing the image of the Colonel. She could feel the scream rising through her body but knew if she started she would never stop.

Looking at the floor she took deep breaths trying to calm herself before looking again at the Colonel who was in the most bizarre situation she could never have imagined. After a few minutes she realised that nothing could be done for him and she backed out of the bathroom.

Somehow she had to get down the stairs. She stretched down a foot to the first step but her legs just wouldn't hold her up and she plumped down onto the top step. From there she bumped down stair by stair on her bottom until she reached the penultimate step.

Luckily for her just within reach through the stair rails was a small hall table where the phone rested. She picked it up but couldn't for the life of her think whom she should call. She knew who she wanted to call. Who she desperately needed but it was impossible. A small address book was lying alongside the phone, she picked it up and started turning the pages until she stopped at the L's then dialled the number and waited.

Chapter Eight -Even Later That Morning - Celia Gets A Call

Celia stood at the sink peeling the potatoes and preparing the vegetables for lunch; the meat was ready to be carved, Ronald's favourite. She'd already cooked the brisket the day before giving it a good 4 hours on a low heat ensuring it would be lovely and tender. With all the veg prepared and the Yorkshire pudding mixed she decided to go and do a spot more of gardening.

She went into Ronald's shed and found her purple flowered gardening gloves 99p from the bargain shop. Putting them on, they weren't very comfortable but as Ronald pointed out cheap and disposable, she headed out into the garden. She did a satisfying hour or so's weeding before going indoors to put the lunch on. The potatoes had just come to the boil and she was turning them down to simmer when the phone rang.

"Hello?"

"Mrs Ladygarden? I'm sorry to disturb you on a Sunday morning, It's Mrs Cottle here."

"Mrs Cottle? hello, what can I do for you?" Celia was surprised, they had never spoken on the phone before.

"It's er, it's er the Colonel. He's had an accident." Her voice broke a little as she forced the words out.

"Oh I am sorry Mrs Cottle, what's happened and what can I do for you?"

"Well actually. He's dead."

"Oh my!" Celia put her hand over the phone and called "Ronald! Come here, quick."

" I'm so sorry to ask but there isn't anybody else. I wondered if you could come around to Apple cottage."

"Oh dear" Celia was taken by surprise but recovered quickly reassuring Mrs Cottle "Well of course I'll come. I'll just put some shoes on and I'll be right there."

Celia only ever saw Mrs Cottle occasionally at Church

and sometimes she was in her garden when Celia walked Hirsute Roley. As far as she knew Mrs Cottle had never attended any of the village activities, unlike her mother-in-law who had been on every committee going when she was alive. Celia was surprised Mrs Cottle had called her for help considering they were still on fairly formal terms instead of some of the other ladies from church. She presumed Mrs Cottle would know them a lot better.

Ronald hadn't heard Celia call and she found him sitting in a sunny spot in the garden wearing his straw hat, reading the Sunday papers with a glass of Guinness.

"Ronald I have to go around to Mrs Cottles. Apparently the Colonel has had an accident and she's asked if I can go around to help."

"What about lunch?"

"Is that all you can think about, the poor woman has lost her husband!"

"Has she? I thought you said he'd had an accident."

"Give me strength, yes, he has had an accident but she says he's dead."

"Dead? Then she needs the undertaker. Why did she call you? We don't know them very well do we?"

"Well no we don't but she's rung me now and she sounded ever so upset so I'll have to go. Look, can you finish cooking the lunch? The potatoes are probably ready to strain. Then when it's ready you'd better eat yours because I'm not sure when I'll be back, just put a plate over mine and I'll eat it later."

"OK, pass on my condolences."

Celia picked up her capacious handbag, popped in her mobile phone, a couple of tissues, checked she had her notebook and pen and headed for the front door. Only to return and collect together some wool and a pair of knitting needles. She grabbed her grey cardigan from the hall stand in case it became chilly later and left her bungalow. Typical just when she was in her scruffy at-home clothes she had to walk around the village and on a Sunday too!

7

CELIA LENDS A HAND

It didn't take Celia long to make her way around the village to the lane where the Cottles lived. She opened the gate and walked down the path. Although nervous as to what she would find in the house, she couldn't help but admire the immaculate garden. Out of the corner of her eye she saw movement at the window of the cottage next door, glancing across she had a fleeting glimpse of pink before it disappeared from view. Pinky being nosy she thought as she rang the bell at the front door of the Cottles cottage.

Celia was curious as to what accident could have happened to the Colonel that could have killed him and she had expected an ambulance or paramedic to be there but it was all very quiet. It wasn't long before she found out as Mrs Cottle had been waiting for Celia's ring and the door opened before Celia could take her finger off the bell and she was ushered inside.

"This is so kind of you Mrs Ladygarden, thank you for coming so quickly,"

"It's fine Mrs Cottle now what can I do to help?"

"I thought you'd be the right sort of person who'd keep calm in a crisis and would know what to do and someone that I could trust."

"You can certainly count on me for that. Has the accident only just happened then?"

"Yes, I think so but I can't be sure, I came home from church and found him dead in the bath."

Celia instantly became suspicious, dead in the bath in the middle of the day, very strange she thought but said "And you're sure he's dead?"

Mrs Cottle's eyes quickly filled with tears and she closed them but quickly opened them again. "Oh yes quite sure."

Celia guessed she was seeing the image of the Colonel lying dead in the bath and asked "What do you think happened to the Colonel?"

"I don't know, I have never seen anything so strange in all my life."

Celia's curiosity was on overdrive but she was well aware that what was strange to some was normal for others. "Was it so strange for him to have a bath in the middle of the day? Perhaps he became hot and sticky mowing the lawn."

"James would never normally leave half a strip of lawn not mown, he was meticulous in everything he did. But that wasn't the only strange thing." Mrs Cottle said.

Celia was fidgeting with impatience and asked sharply. "What was so strange?"

Mrs Cottle looked at Celia.

Celia apologised "Sorry, carry on in your own time."

"He was lying in the bath with the lawnmower on top of him." Mrs Cottle said looking at Celia.

"Well the first thing we must do is call the police." Stated Celia.

"The police? But surely the doctor would be better."

"If you think he's dead it's probably a bit late for that but don't worry Mrs Cottle I'll call the doctor as well. You leave it to me, why don't you go and sit down and as soon as I've made these calls, I'll make us a nice cup of tea. There isn't anything you can do at present. Is there any family I can call for you as well?"

"No there was only me and James."

Celia was feeling a bit wobbly as it wasn't every day you were called in to deal with a sudden death. It wasn't the standard domestic emergency such as lending a bag of flour or taking a parcel in. She went across the hall to use the phone thinking how sad that Mrs Cottle didn't have any family close by and had to rely on acquaintances at a time like this. She was curious to know more about the Cottles.

She glanced up the stairs as she dialled the surgery and after listening to a recorded message that seemed to go on for hours was given an emergency number to ring. Oh bugger that thought Celia and dialled a local number.

"Oh hi Gill, sorry to bother you on a Sunday but is Ken there? Gill! you know I wouldn't bother him unless it was an emergency. No I'm fine and so is Ronald. I'm afraid I can't tell you what it's about but if I could speak to Ken urgently please. Hello Ken, sorry about this but do you know the Cottles who live in Apple Cottage, used to be Major and Mrs Cottle's and before them old Miss Spence's. That's right, well Colonel Cottle has had an accident..."

"You should have rung the doctor's emergency number or if it's a really bad accident then call for an ambulance. You shouldn't be bothering me on a Sunday Celia. This is the trouble living in a small village everyone thinks they can call me out every five minutes.!"

"If you've quite finished Ken. I am *really* sorry to bother you and you should know I wouldn't under normal circumstances but Mrs Cottle says the Colonel is dead. I am just about to call the Police but wondered if you would come over in the meantime, you know how long they take. You will? OK see you in five minutes."

Celia had brought her mobile phone into the hall with her, not sure what number to call the police on she looked up North Devon Police on Google. The first question on the website was 'Do you need to call 101?' Well I don't know thought Celia, do I? The second instruction was '#ClickB4UCall' - Online options for non urgent matters. Was it urgent? Probably not, thought Celia but she knew that the police must attend any sudden deaths. We also encourage you to use the 'Ask the Police online facility for commonly asked questions'. Celia wondered if they had a question for 'What to do when a person dies unexpectedly in the bath in the middle of a Sunday' with a lawnmower on top of them. Underneath this was a series of cheerful icons wearing police hats. Then, NON EMERGENCY - If a crime has happened use the online crime reporting form.

Celia gave up, if she dialled 101 she would get the same problem as she had ringing the surgery, a long wait and lots of options. She went to her contacts and looked in the B's then tapped.

"Hi Audrey, sorry to bother you on a Sunday but I wonder if you would get a message to Billy for me. Great. Keep this to yourself please Audrey but tell him that Colonel Cottle has died and to go to Apple Cottage, in St

Uriths as soon as he can. Can't really tell you anything else yet Audrey but I will be waiting for him."

Billy would be able to contact the police far quicker than Celia could. At least they still had a local police station even if it was on reduced hours but according to last night's, news, even that was going to close. It looked like they were going the same way as the cottage hospitals.

Celia went back into the kitchen to find Mrs Cottle staring into space as she sat at the table. She lifted the kettle and finding water in it switched it on. "Where are the mugs Mrs Cottle?" asked Celia, but she didn't have time to make tea as just then the doorbell rang.

"Why don't you go up to your room and rest Mrs Cottle, I'll deal with the authorities, then I'll make tea."

Celia waited till Mrs Cottle had gone upstairs then opened the front door to Doctor Frobisher's ring. "Come in Ken and go straight up, the Colonel is upstairs in the bathroom."

"Have you been up and checked him Celia?"

"No Ken, Mrs Cottle was convinced he was dead and when she said he was in the bath in the middle of the day and then there was the lawnmower, I thought it might be a police matter and I shouldn't contaminate the scene."

Dr Frobisher gave her a puzzled look "I think you've been reading too many murder mysteries Celia." Grabbing the newel post and starting up the stairs, he called over his shoulder "call the police Celia there's a good girl."

Making a double two-finger dance to the doctor's back Celia managed to squeeze the words out between gritted teeth assuring the dinosaur doctor that she had called the police before calling him.

8

BILLY TO THE RESCUE

PCSO Boy rang the doorbell and popped his head around the open front door.

"Hello! Anyone there?"

"Come in Billy"

"Hello Mrs L, shame about the poor old Colonel. Doctor here is he?"

"Yes Billy, he's with the Colonel now"

"Is he? I thought he was dead"

"He is dead Billy, the doctor is confirming this"

"Right you are, I came as soon as mum called me because I was already in the village. I'll call in the real police if I need to when I've spoken to the doctor. Shall I pop the kettle on Mrs L? Cup of tea always makes things better, my mum always says."

Secretly thinking that Billy would have fitted into the 1950's quite easily with his old-fashioned chirpy way of speaking Celia said "She is absolutely right Billy but you *are* a real policeman so that being the case shouldn't you be following police procedure and securing the scene?"

"What scene?"

"The scene of the death of course."

"Oh crikey! Do I have to do that, I thought that was only in the event of a suspicious death."

"You're probably not up to that page in the PCSO Manual. "

"Steady on Mrs L, I take my job very seriously."

Celia patiently said "well we don't know what sort of death it was yet do we Billy, except for the fact it is an unexplained and sudden death?"

"I hadn't thought of that, I just thought because he was old, it must have been natural causes like." Billy paused "Mrs L now we're on proper police business, couldn't you drop the Billy and give me my real title of PCSO Boy?"

"Sorry Billy, you're right, you deserve my respect but hang on a minute, the Colonel was hardly old he was only in his 40's and you do know how the Colonel died don't you?"

"Of course Mrs L, I have the message saved on my ipad." Switching on the tablet and looking important Billy read out. "The male deceased one Colonel Cottle who resided at Apple Cottage in the village of St Urith Without Well, on Sunday 28th of July, died mowing the lawn with his electric lawnmower."

"Not quite Billy, 'Colonel', 'died' and 'lawnmower' feature but I think you have the plot wrong. How do you know about the lawnmower, I didn't mention it to your mother?"

"Mum told Betty Bins about your call and she told mum that Ruby had been watching the Colonel mowing his lawn as usual this morning but little Bertie dropped his millett. By the time she'd picked it up and clipped it back on his cage, then looked out again, the Colonel hadn't finished his lawn but he was gone and so was the lawnmower." Explained Billy.

Trust Ruby to know what was going on in the village thought Celia. "I did tell your mum to keep it to herself!. Go on then up you go PCSO Boy and join the doctor in the bathroom."

"I beg your pardon Mrs L; I won't be joining anyone in the bathroom!"

"Billy stop acting like a prim miss in a Victorian melodrama, the Colonel is in the bathroom as well"

Billy was by now completely confused asked "But how did he get there? And what about the Lawnmower?"

Celia knowing that what she was about to say, could tip Billy over the edge said gently "Billy the lawnmower is in the bathroom."

Billy, suddenly concerned placed his hand on Celia's arm "I say steady on Mrs L, have we been sharing one or two too many with Ronald this morning?"

"Billy! Get up those stairs and check out the crime scene, before heaven help us the Inspector arrives and chews your ear off for not doing it."

"Right you are Mrs L" Billy was puzzled but not brave enough to argue with Celia who had known him since he was a kid and more importantly was friends with his mother; tentatively he climbed the stairs not quite suppressing his usual puppy bounciness. As he reached the landing, the doctor was just coming out of the bathroom. He could see Mrs Cottle through her bedroom door, she had taken Celia's advice and had been resting on the bed.

"Hi Doc what's happened here then?" Billy asked quietly.

"Well young Billy, I think you should take a good look.

At this stage I'm not sure what has happened exactly, it's all very odd. It appears the Colonel was cleaning his electric lawnmower in the bath. Not a wise decision. Water and electricity is a lethal mix, the results were inevitable."

"Perhaps I'd better call the Inspector and wait he gets here, I don't want to contaminate the scene."

"Bit dramatic young Billy, you've been watching too many police programmes on the telly. Bit of an odd situation I'll grant you but I'm almost sure a simple accident is what we have here. I shall have to have a word with my lady wife. She always puts the whisk ends of her handmixer in the washing up bowl and switches them on to clean the cake mixture off. Probably not a good idea in light of what's happened here today. But you do your duty lad and wait for the Inspector. We'd better follow the rules."

Stifling his irritation at being called young Billy and lad but that's what you get when you've lived in the same village all your life, he stepped to one side allowing the doctor access to the stairs. With considerable trepidation, bearing in mind it was a Sunday and *nobody ever called the Inspector on a Sunday*, he radioed in a call for the Inspector. He desperately hoped that the inspector may have reached the 19th hole by the time he received the call.

Being a kind and well brought up young man, he gently knocked on Mrs Cottle's bedroom door. "Mrs C? I'm really sorry about the Colonel, do you feel up to joining me and Mrs L for a cup of tea? Might make you feel better."

Mrs Cottle couldn't help but smile at Billy's naivety but she appreciated his good intentions. "That's a splendid idea Billy ". Wiping her eyes with an embroidered cotton handkerchief, she rose from her bed. She glanced at the bathroom door as she passed and an involuntary shudder ran through her; Billy patted her arm in a comforting way and Mrs Cottle thought what a kind and sensitive boy he was.

Celia and the doctor were already sat at the kitchen table when Mrs Cottle and Billy entered.

"Tea everyone?" Celia stood up, crossed to the counter and flicked the switch on the electric kettle. She had already warmed the pot and laid out cups and saucers as she hadn't been able to find any mugs.

"Not really a tea drinker my dear, any chance of a little nip of whisky, I'm sure the Colonel wouldn't mind?" Dr Frobisher inclined his head to Mrs Cottle.

"Of course doctor, Billy would you mind?"

"I don't mind Mrs C, if the doctor wants a drink it's OK by me." Billy puffed out his chest self- importantly.

Celia and Dotty shared a smile then Celia asked "Billy would you be a dear and fetch the doctor a whisky?"

"Righto Mrs L, where's it to?"

"The key to the Tantalus is on the top shelf of the bookcase under Michael Jackson's 'Whisky'" Mrs Cottle said.

"Oh My God! You've got Michael Jackson's whisky" Billy's eyes were huge "and a Tarantula?"

Mrs Cottle and the doctor looked at Billy as if he had gone mad so Celia seized the moment and Billy's arm hauling him out of the kitchen "c'mon Billy I'll show you." She shepherded the babbling PCSO Boy into the dining room.

"How come they've got Michael Jackson's whisky? Did they buy it at an auction?"

"They haven't Billy, it's a book written by Michael Jackson about whisky."

"Wow I thought he only wrote songs, it just goes to show, you think you know everything."

Celia managed to conceal her amusement. Billy wasn't stupid he was just short on life experience. "Different Michael Jackson Billy." Celia carefully pulled out the 'Malt Whisky Companion' opening the book to reveal the key in the secret compartment.

"That's amazing, it looks like a proper book. It's a great way of hiding things. You could put all sorts of important things in there, like a passport. It's like something off Dragon's Den, I love that programme, I'm always trying to think of new things to invent. Don't know what a tarantler is though."

"Goodness you're getting an education this morning Billy." Replied Celia. "The word is Tantalus and is rather outdated these days. It comes from the times when the rich locked up their spirits to stop the servants stealing it."

Billy followed Celia across to the polished oak sideboard where she inserted the key into the lock of the Tantalus. A beautifully crafted mahogany example with silver decoration. Celia unlocked it removing the Whisky. She bent down to open the sideboard door looking for a glass when Billy asked.

"I don't understand, why would the Colonel lock up his whisky?"

"I don't know, as I said it's quite an old fashioned thing to do, I think it must have been one of the Colonels 'little ways.' Mrs Cottle doesn't strike me as a secret drinker but I am never surprised to find that nearly everyone has secrets Billy."

"I haven't Mrs L, an open book me."

Celia looked at him whilst she held the bottle in one hand and the glass in the other.

"Really? A little bird tells me you are getting quite an addiction to buns lately."

Try as he might Billy could not control the pink flush that climbed relentlessly up from his neck until it covered every bit of his face clashing beautifully with his carrot-coloured hair.

Celia carefully poured two fingers of whisky into the glass and made her way back to the kitchen.

Following on behind, Billy slightly bemused said quietly to himself "How does Celia find out everyone's secrets." Celia turned her head, smiled and winked at him.

There was an uneasy quiet in the kitchen, everyone had run out of things to say but nobody could relax except for Dr Frobisher who was on his second whisky. They all jumped when there was a fierce knocking on the front door.

PCSO Boy jumped to his feet. "That'll be the boss." He tore out of the kitchen knocking the handle of a china jug with his elbow in his haste. It teetered, looked as if it was going to right itself before it leaped off the edge. Celia a keen member of the rounder's team in her youth, stuck out her hand and surprised everyone by deftly catching it and placing it back on the dresser, whilst Mrs Cottle and the doctor were still in mid-gasp.

9

AN INSPECTOR CALLS

Murmured conversation drifted back at them from the hall with the odd sharp-noted word. Celia strained to hear.

"What? Some bloody interfering woman!" mumble mumble "bloody Sunday morning " mumble mumble. The bulk of Inspector Dunster filled the kitchen doorway.

Shortarse with an ego taller than himself, came to Celia's mind when observing the Inspector.

The Inspector looked into the kitchen but didn't make eye contact with either woman and said "Mrs Cottle?"

She half rose from her chair but the inspector waved her down. "Ok ma'am, sit down for now." He gave Celia a hard stare as if to say, 'you are the reason I'm missing my golf,' then he barked at the Doctor.

"Come on doctor, let's get this over with, it had better be worth pulling me away from the 17th on a Sunday for."

Celia thought that If anyone was in any doubt as to the inspector's activity prior to this visit, one glance at his outfit would not only have told the whole story but illustrated it as well. The jumper held a pattern of large connecting diamonds on the front in a shade of green that could only be described as acidic a bit like the Inspector's nature. This was worn over a pair of bright yellow checked 'Rupert Bear' trousers with the bottoms tucked into some Argyle socks. The whole lot was topped off with a canary yellow peaked cap which unfortunately accentuated the inspectors protruding comedy ears.

Downing the last few drops of whisky the doctor stood on slightly unsteady legs an indication that he had possibly already had one or two pre-lunch Sherries before arriving at the Cottles cottage.

"Yes of course Inspector, follow me" he tried to squeeze past the Inspector's bulk but had to wait until the Inspector stepped back allowing him through. Leading the way up the stairs the doctor stopped on the landing and pointed to the bathroom door. "He's in there."

Inspector Burke pushed the door open and stepped inside "good God!" after the expected few seconds of silence. The inspector his face a mixture of shock and surprise joined the doctor on the landing. "Bad business this doctor. Of course I've seen it all before."

"Really? You do surprise me Inspector."

Puffing himself up with self-importance the Inspector replied "oh yes, I've seen it all doc. If I had a pound for every sex-game gone wrong, I'd be a rich man."

"Really inspector you do surprise me but I thought it was a straightforward accident. I mean isn't it unusual to play a sex-game with a lawnmower? In the bath?"

"Well yes I take your point. No I'll admit the lawnmower is a first for me." Agreed the Inspector.

"And he *was* fully clothed." Added the Doctor.

"Very bizarre, I give you that. But typical of a public

school ex-army chap, they always like to make a show" the inspector said with a superior smile.

"Well I bow to your superior knowledge. So you definitely think it's an accident do you?" Asked the doctor.

"Definitely. Clear- cut case."

"And you don't you think the setup is at all a little bit odd?" the doctor persisted.

"Well yes as I've already said it is a little unusual" replied the Inspector getting irritated at the doctors persistence.

More than a little unusual thought the doctor but the Inspector seems convinced. He may be a puffed up ninny but he is the expert so he must know what he's doing.

The inspector tried to put an arm around the doctor's shoulders in a chummy way but as he was at least ten inches shorter than the doctor, he fell short and he had to make do with a pat on the back.

"Doctor, don't you think it would be a kindness to put the cause of death as an accident to spare the little woman?"

"Pompous little twit." thought the doctor. If I referred to my wife as 'the little woman' I'd certainly know all about it. I'd be walking with a limp for a month. The lady wife is a far more acceptable term.

"Well if you say so inspector. You'll confirm that in your report will you?"

"Yes, yes. Tell Mrs Cottle she can call in the funeral directors. I'll get PCSO Boy to remove the lawnmower. I don't know why that bloody woman interfered and got the PCSO to call me in. If he hadn't been so wet behind the ears he could have dealt with it.Never mind I can be back on the green within the hour."

"Well if you're happy Inspector, I'll write out the death certificate."

"Not sure if happy is the right expression in the circs doc but I get your drift."

"No quite, mmm, yes I'll er..." Doctor Frobisher made his escape down the stairs and into the dining room to complete his paperwork accompanied by another steadying whisky.

The Inspector stood in the hall and beckoned PCSO Boy from the kitchen doorway.

"Right Boy, fetch that lawnmower down and put it away in the shed if there is one, out of Mrs Cottles sight. Wait a minute did *you* pull the lawnmower plug out of the socket?"

"Nno ssir, it was already out when I got here" stuttered Billy. This was the first time he had spoken to the Inspector; his reputation in the station had been enough to ensure Billy had kept well out of his way. He hadn't expected to come across any dead people when he had joined the force, a little light local theft and missing pets was what he had in mind. But PCSO Boy was made of stern stuff even if he wasn't aware of it yet. A bright young man with a lot of common sense, if he wasn't too nervous to use it.

"Shall I take some photographs of the scene before I disturb it sir?"

"Hurry up now, get a jiggle on. Whoa what did you just say Boy?"

"Sorry sir, I just thought..."

"Well don't. That's my job! Now do as you're told and get cracking." Turning, the Inspector walked into the kitchen to speak to Mrs Cottle.

"I'm sorry for your loss ma'am. I have thoroughly

investigated the situation and I am positive that your husband died as the result of an accident. We think he was attempting to clean off the lawnmower blades and he used the bath as obviously the sink would have been too small. If you can imagine the scene…"

Mrs Cottle turned pale as she did indeed picture the scene.

"When I'm baking a cake, I beat the butter and the sugar until they are creamed to perfection. Then I carefully add the beaten eggs, fold in the flour…" The Inspector's said, his eyes sparkling with enthusiasm as he gazed into the distance, picturing the scene in his head.

Celia cleared her throat. "arrghum."

Inspector Burke gave Celia a dark look. "Well what I was trying to explain was that I lift the food mixer whisks up in the bowl just enough to fling off the cake mixture. Well that's obviously what your husband must have tried. It was the doctor who put me on the right track. Colonel Cottle plugged the lawnmower in and switched it on so that the blades would fling off the grass under the water. Obviously with disastrous consequences. Right well that's all from us, you can call in the funeral directors now. Goodbye ma'am."

Celia stood up, astonished by the inspectors description of cake making in his explanation of the Colonel's bizarre death. But before she could gather her thoughts or comment on what he had said. The inspector had walked briskly out of the kitchen, through the front door, slamming it behind him. The mirage of the green and yellow ensemble he had worn hovered in the air.

10

BILLY GOES ALL CSI

Billy Boy climbed the stairs slowly and stopped when he arrived at the landing. Preparing himself for the worst, he walked across the landing to the bathroom door. Standing in the doorway he pulled out his mobile phone, quickly snapping off a few pictures. He was a serious NCIS fan and whenever they arrived at a scene that was the first thing they did.

Knowing he didn't have long he scanned the scene for any clues. It was a very traditional bathroom or old-fashioned as Billy thought. There were black and white square tiles on the floor, white tiles around the deep bath and at the back of the wash basin.

The toilet was similar to the one Pinky-Pope had in his back garden, with a cistern up high on the wall and a chain with a handle to pull on the end. Billy knew this because when he was still at school he used to help Pinky dig his garden for pocket money.

Above the sink was a white gloss-painted cupboard with a round mirror on the door. The last thing he wanted to look at was the body of the colonel in the bath but he knew he had to. But as he stepped towards it he spotted something on the floor near the bath. Squatting down to look, he saw two small separate piles of dirt that were reddish streaked with yellow, possibly where two feet had stood .

He took out a plastic evidence bag from his pocket, he always carried some just in case but this is the first time he'd had the opportunity to use them. They weren't proper evidence bags, they were bags that had contained beads or lace that were delivered to his mum.

Standing up he opened the bathroom cabinet and rummaged around until he found a box of haemorrhoid capsules. He tore off the end of the box and put it back in the cupboard. Tearing the piece of cardboard in half he squatted down again and carefully slid the two pieces of card towards each other fetching up as much of the dirt as possible and poured it into the plastic evidence bag. After he'd sealed the bag he wrote on it using a felt tip pen and tucked it into his pocket.

He stepped back close to the bath and looked down. This was his first dead body and looking down at the Colonel, now a sickly shade of green, he was more curious than upset. It really was a freaky way to die. As Billy took in the prunation of his fingers, the sickly shade of green, the burn marks and blistered areas on the Colonel's torso where the lawnmower blades had rested against flesh, his insides suddenly contracted and his legs disappeared from under him causing him to sit down suddenly on the floor. Phew! Obviously the body was freaking him out more than he thought. 'Buck up Billy.' Did he really just say that out loud? But the sentiment was right. He stood up and tested his legs, yes they were working.

He picked up the plug end of the electric cord and wound it up then laid it down again as he realised the lawnmower would drip everywhere, plus he didn't want Mrs C to see the lawnmower when he took it out if the house. Digging into the old fashioned ali-baba laundry basket which made him feel a bit icky, he found a large bath towel and laid it out on the floor. Grabbing the handle in one hand and trying not to touch the body, the bottom of the mower in the other he lifted out the dripping machine and sat it on the towel, wrapping it around before taking it downstairs and out of the front door preventing Mrs Cottle seeing it.

Taking it around the side of the house and into the back garden he wasn't sure where to put the damn thing. He didn't think it should go in the shed like the inspector said because he knew it wouldn't work again but he didn't want to put it by the recycling bin where Mrs C could see it and then she would have to get it out to the front pavement for the recyclers to collect. The towel was now wet and dripping onto his uniform and he couldn't help thinking that this water had been swirling around the Colonel. I need to put it down but perhaps it should be kept for evidence he thought.

Whilst he stood dithering Celia came out of the back door. "Well young Billy what are you going to do with that?"

"God Mrs L you made me jump, I'm not sure what's gone on here but something doesn't feel quite right to me. The Inspector told me to put this back in the shed. I don't want to leave it here for Mrs C to find but I don't want to hold on to it any longer either!"

His habit of calling everyone by their initial he had absorbed from his mother and although it was irritating in her it was rather endearing in young Billy thought Celia.

"Quite right Billy always trust your gut feeling. Why don't you pop it round to my place? Tell Ronald I said he was to put it in the shed but not to touch it. She poked her head in the shed which was extremely tidy and spotted a plastic cover. "Here Billy, let's get rid of that soggy towel, we'll cover it in this and why don't you take it around in the Colonel's wheelbarrow."

"Right-Oh Mrs L that's a good idea."

Celia watched Billy set off around the side of the cottage, struggling a bit until he got the weight of the mower right. That boy is brighter than he looks and that stupid inspector couldn't spot a murder even if a hissing Hannibal Lecter came to dinner and a family member had disappeared every time he looked up from his plate!

Mrs Cottle and Celia sat quietly at the kitchen table chatting about the weather, their gardens and general goings on in the village until Celia said " You mentioned that you don't any have family in England. So does that mean you have family living abroad?"

"I erm." Mrs Cottle stuttered. Just then the doorbell rang. "Oh that will be the funeral directors." She began to rise.

Celia recognised a relieved face when she saw one and wondered what Dottie was hiding. "It's Ok I'll go." She went to the front door and opened it. "Come in Mr Speedwell, Lexie."

G.Speedwell & Son are a well respected local family firm of funeral directors and were well known to both of the ladies.

Celia led them into the kitchen and they all sat down around the table. Isn't it funny that everyone always gather in the kitchen instead of the sitting room. Probably a comfort thing. She thought Mrs Cottle would normally have taken everyone through to the sitting room but she looked as though she didn't have the energy to do anything about it.

"Mrs Cottle, we are so sorry for your loss, we will do anything in our power to help you through this difficult time."

"Thank you Gerald, do I have to do anything now?"

"Not for now. If you are ready we'll take the colonel to our chapel of rest and then myself or Lexie will come back and see you again in a couple of days."

"Thank you." Mrs Cottle rose from her chair as a sign to the Speedwells that they could carry on.

When the Speedwells had left with the Colonel's body Mrs Cottle said to Celia "I think I'm going to go up and have a lie down again for a little while if you don't mind."

"Of course not, I'll stay here until you wake up shall I?"

"Would you mind, I know it's a lot to ask but I would rest easier."

"You go on up, I'll be fine."

Celia waited until she heard Mrs Cottle go up the stairs then reached for her handbag. She intended to have a go at her knitting as she wasn't one who could just sit and do nothing. She was never usually far from a pair of knitting needles and wool, she always liked to have some project on the go. As she rummaged around in her capacious bag she found the other thing that she always carried around with her, a notebook, pulling it out along with the pen that was attached.

11

CELIA GETS TO THINKING - JUST AFTER LUNCHTIME

Opening a clean page Celia stared out of the Cottles kitchen window not really seeing the neat rows of produce in the vegetable patch or the abundant crop in the purpose built fruit cage but musing on the day's events.

How rude of the Inspector, he didn't even acknowledge me, let alone speak to me and I don't care what that stupid man thinks, I think the Colonel was murdered. A frisson of excitement travelled from Celia's electric blue varnished toenails right up to the top of her blonde highlighted hair. Even her ears felt as if they were tingling. She needed to organise the myriad things floating around in her brain, so she started writing a list. She was a great one for lists.

1. Why did the Colonel stop mowing in the middle of a row?
2. Why would the Colonel get into a bathful of water with all his clothes on?
3. What caused the trauma to the back of his

head (the doctor had mentioned this after his second whisky)?
4. Why did an intelligent man try and clean an electric lawnmower in the bath?
5. Why was the Colonel lying on his back? If he really was washing the lawnmower wouldn't he be standing up leaning over the bath and therefore would have fallen face down in the bath?
6. Who would want the Colonel dead?
7. Why wasn't the widow as distraught as might be expected (she was clearly shocked but?)
8. Why did the Inspector insist on suicide
9. What did Billy Boy find in the bathroom
10. Who pulled the electric plug out

Celia's note number 9 made her itch to get into the bathroom and have a look around for herself, Mrs Cottle was having a little nap;this was the perfect time.

I'll just have a little peek, Celia thought. As she passed the floor to ceiling oak dresser she noticed the large china jug that Billy had nearly sent to the dustbin in bits. Celia liked china jugs and had a modest collection. This was definitely not an English jug she thought. Turning it over to see what the bottom revealed, a postcard fluttered out and dropped on to the floor. The Jug had been made in Greece. She picked up the postcard and looked at the picture of a Greek village scene on it. It looked like a recent postcard but there was no postmark or address so it must have been sent in an envelope.

'My darling, I am writing this sitting on the terrace of our taverna underneath the mulberry trees. Every day you are not here with me on our island feels like a week, every week like a month. I will not wait much longer. Your Nico.'

Very curious thought Celia. Who was Nico. And more importantly who was he writing too? It seemed too far fetched to think that the jug had the postcard in it when it was bought unless it had been bought second hand. The first thing anybody would do is look inside, Celia reasoned. So who was this postcard sent to? She put it back in the jug where she'd found it. Then added a note to her list.

11. Who was Nico? And who was he writing too?

She climbed the stairs quietly on tight feet, well not tight feet, feet with tights on. One doesn't say stockinged feet anymore unless it was in an Agatha Christie novel. Creeping up the stairs she thought how glad she was to live in a bungalow, her knees didn't like these stairs at all. Stopping at the top she listened but heard no sound, she glanced back at Mrs Cottles bedroom door before grasping the knob on the bathroom door. She turned it slowly and gently pushed it open.

"Mrs Ladygarden!"

"Shiiii...sugar!" Celia started.

"Sorry, I didn't mean to make you jump, did you want to use the toilet? I've just finished cleaning it."

Celia observed the yellow rubber-gloves, the bleach, diminished kitchen roll and the newly widowed Mrs Cottle sitting on the closed toilet seat.

"Mrs Cottle you didn't have to do this, I would have done it for you."

"Celia why don't you call me Dottie?"

"You're not that bad, I mean it's perfectly OK, the shock and everything."

"No I'm not saying I'm dotty, I'm saying my name is

Dorothy but I prefer to be called Dottie and as we find ourselves in a difficult situation and you have been such a support, it seems sensible to use our first names."

"Yes of course Dottie, now can I finish off in here for you?"

"No I've finished, I was just sitting here thinking."

"Understandable but wouldn't you be better out of this room?"

"You're right of course, I'll put all this in the bin and we'll have a fresh pot of tea if you can stomach another one and Celia, thank you."

"Don't you worry about..."

"Ssh I mean it. Thank you for your support and for staying here today, goodness knows what your husband must be thinking."

"Don't worry about Ronald he's used to me going off here and there at the drop of a hat. I'll take that, you go and put the kettle on." Celia took the black plastic dustbin bag out of Dottie's hands and went down the stairs in front of her, through the kitchen and out of the back door. When she was out of sight of the kitchen window, Celia struggled to untie the knot in the bag before peering inside. What she saw surprised her, it was all of the Colonels toiletries, medicines and a razor. It seemed to Celia a little soon to clear out his things but then everyone is different. Tying the bag back up she put it in the shed thinking that Dottie would put it out on dustbin day.

Back in the kitchen, Dottie was putting out a different set of cups and saucers and Celia recognised the pattern as Prince Albert. Her own mother had had a tea set of the same. Whilst the tea was brewing in the matching teapot, Celia was musing on what tea-cosy pattern would fit the unusual shape. She would have a look at some of her vintage patterns as the one she often used was for the more common round brown teapot.

Dottie opened the pantry door disappearing inside and returning with a bright orange 'Celebrations' tub.

"Ooh chocolates" Celia's eyes lit up. She was rather partial to chocolate at any time and her tummy was reminding her that she'd missed her lunch and hadn't eaten since breakfast.

"No sorry it's carrot-cake. Would you rather have a chocolate, I think I have a box somewhere."

"No carrot-cake will be lovely, thank you, it's my favourite."

Cutting a generous slice Dottie placed it on a matching tea plate and pushed it across the table towards Celia.

"Are you going to have some? You ought to eat something even if you don't feel like it." Celia suggested through a mouthful of cake.

Dottie poured out the tea "Perhaps a small piece would be a good idea." She cut herself a piece of cake which even to Celia's idea of generous portions it wasn't that small. When Dottie devoured the cake in a few short bites a tiny little niggle buried itself in her consciousness.

"Why haven't we done this before Celia. What a shame it has taken a death to bring us together."

Celia didn't like to point out that up until now Dottie had kept herself to herself apart from an occasional 'good morning' when she had been walking past with hirsute Roley. Some people like Dottie found it hard to go out on their own socially to village events or to the social club and the Colonel had been away for long periods at a time. Now that he was retired they still didn't join in very much. Celia felt that now Dottie was widowed, she should make an effort to go out and meet people. She was glad that she herself had a large circle of friends that she could rely on.

"It's never too late Dottie, we must make an effort to meet up occasionally, perhaps you'd like to come to our monthly craft group? We get up to all sorts of things, some knit, some paint, some crochet, you can even just sit, chat, drink tea and eat cake if you want."

"It sounds lovely Celia and I might be able to come to one or two but I won't be staying here now that the Colonel has gone."

" Perhaps it's a little early to make important decisions Dottie; you must give yourself some time to come to terms with your loss."

"You may be right but I *have* made up my mind."

Celia finished her tea puzzled and slightly uncomfortable in the silence following Dottie's statement whilst Dottie started to collect up the tea things.

"Celia please don't take offence but I think I'd like to be on my own now. You have been so kind to stay and I cannot thank you enough for your support."

"Dottie of course, don't worry about it. I'll pop off now, of course you need some time to yourself."

Celia stood up and gathered together her cardigan from the back of the chair and her

handbag from under the table.

"I'm only a phone call away, give me a ring any time if you need anything at all, won't you?"

"I will, bye Celia and thank you." Dottie followed Celia to the door and closed it quietly behind her.

12

COLONEL COTTLE - BACK ALONG

Colonel Cottle stood back and admired his 1952 Bentley Continental. He appreciated the styling by Stanley Watts who had been influenced by aerodynamics. The Colonel's drophead R type version had coachwork by Park Ward and he loved the tail fins which stabilised the car at high speeds. A good deal of his time was spent cleaning and polishing the car. In fact the car was probably the only thing in his life he had ever really loved.

This particular morning he grumpily laid out the blue plastic sheet in the boot. Making sure he had folded the corners carefully so that the excess covered the sides as he couldn't allow a speck of foreign material in contact with his beloved car. He wasn't at all happy with the new cheap blue plastic but his old tarpaulin had become stiff and unwieldy. A bit like his marriage to Mrs Cottle.

Using a pair of good quality gardening gloves (no cheap ones for him), he picked up the first green garden bag loaded with cuttings, twigs and branches. There weren't so many as it was summer and it had only been a quick tidy up operation. He loaded the bag into the top right-hand corner of the boot. The other bags followed all carefully stacked against each other. He was just covering them up with a second smaller plastic cover when Dottie called to him.

"Would you take these with you to the dump please?"

Pulling his head out from under the boot lid he looked at what Dottie was holding out, two plastic carrier bags, full to bursting. Why does she insist on overstuffing the bag? He thought. There should be at the very least a four inch gap from the top of the bag. "What's in them and it isn't the dump it's the recycling centre."

"Just some old clothes I don't want anymore." Dottie replied

"I can't take them this time Dottie I'm taking the garden cuttings."

"Just tuck them in on top of them, it's only a couple of bags."

"No I can't because the boot is full and I'm taking the cuttings to the garden waste section."

"Well I'll just pop them on the passenger seat then." Dottie said as she moved away from the back of the car swinging the offending bags. The Colonel just had time to run around in front of her before she reached the handle to the passenger door.

"Give them to me, I'll fit them in somewhere." he said grumpily taking the offending bags.

Dottie was smiling to herself as she walked back to the house.

It took the Colonel another five minutes to fit the two bags into the boot to his exacting standards and he wasn't happy about it.. Finally satisfied that everything was packed in properly he took off his gloves, pulling off one finger at a time, folded them and tucked them into a side pocket before closing the lid.

Sliding onto the tan-leather seats he felt that familiar frisson of excitement that never failed him when he sat in his car. An effect that only one woman had ever had on him. It wasn't Dottie. Not that he wasn't fond of her but.

As his hands caressed the steering wheel, the drive had its usual effect of lifting his mood. Thinking about Dottie's extra bags the Colonel reflected on her. She was a good wife he had always been able to rely on her to keep everything ship shape on the home front when he'd been serving away.

He hadn't allowed her to use his beloved Bentley of course and once, when he had returned home on leave he had been considerably shaken to find she had bought herself a Renault Clio. Without even asking his permission. Even when he had protested that he couldn't see a need for her to have her own car and pointed out that there was a shop and a post office in the village, he couldn't remember getting a response. Somehow Dottie's car had become a fixture.

The Colonel liked to think he ran his home like a well honed unit. He certainly did when his mother was alive and it suited them both. He had tried to maintain those standards when he married Dottie even though he knew there would be adjustments to be made. He had thought she would soon get to know the rules and the way he liked things run. Instead it had been him who'd had to change not Dottie.

He would find himself unloading the dishwasher, surely Dottie's job but sometimes it was the only way he could find his special cup for coffee. Although he had tried just taking his cup out, it drove him mad knowing that the rest were just sitting there waiting to be put away. His cup seemed to be permanently in the dishwasher and when it needed to be emptied Dottie was nowhere to be found and he ended up putting everything away down to the last cup and plate. If that wasn't bad enough, when it was time for his supper of six water biscuits and cheddar cheese cut into regimental soldiers, Dottie had taken to having a long soak in the bath and he'd had no choice but to get it for himself. Standards were slipping and he seemed to have lost all control.

Dottie often didn't seem to hear when he called her, said she was hard of hearing but she had always been able to relate the juiciest snippets of gossip she'd heard while shopping in the village. Although he enjoyed hearing the gossip he wondered if she really did have poor hearing.

What had just happened was a prime example of one of the things that annoyed him, two unplanned bags of clothes!

His heart-rate bumped up a notch and a flush came to his slightly chubby cheeks as he approached the recycling centre. A tumble of excited anticipation swirled around his stomach. Being a man who thought of himself as self-disciplined and in control this was a new experience.

Glancing at his reflection in the driver's mirror he smoothed down the hair on his head and upper lip and smiled realising that he was enjoying this feeling of excitement. There hadn't been much of it since leaving the army, except for his run-ins with some little pipsqueak on the village hall committee. He unfortunately lived next door and in the Colonel's opinion, might be batting for the wrong side as he had taken to wearing pink of all things!

No this feeling was altogether different from anything

he had experienced before. Apart from the palpitations, sweating and flushing there was a distinct stirring in the trouser department. Sex was something he had put a stop to many years ago as being too unpredictable, too messy and not worth the effort involved. He certainly hadn't missed it and he assumed Dottie felt the same way as she had never asked why he'd stopped coming to her room. In fact it was a huge relief as he didn't understand Dottie, she seemed to change during these activities and was unusually demanding. He had felt completely out of control, so he had put a stop to it very soon after they were married.

The sun was shining as he turned into the gates of the recycling centre and the heat was shimmering above the tarmac. Damn and blast it thought the Colonel as he saw several vehicles parked all higgledy-piggledy in no sort of order at all. His Bentley had to be parked well away from the other cars as he didn't want to risk a scratch by being closer, but this also meant that he was further away from the large containers. Switching off the engine he looked across the yard to see if she was working today.

When he'd first noticed the woman some weeks ago she'd been manhandling a large square UPVC window across the yard. He must have been staring at her because the other woman who worked there spoke at his shoulder "she's building her own house that's why she's taking the window."

"Hasn't she got a builder?" asked the Colonel.

"No she doesn't need one, she's building it out of car tires. She wants to build it herself, she's amazing." The woman walked away towards the rusty old container that served as an office.

The Colonel had been fascinated. This was a whole new world; he couldn't ever imagine Dottie building her own house but then he couldn't imagine building one himself either! He had watched as the two women stood together drinking tea out of mugs at their makeshift office, he hadn't been able to take his eyes off them. Both nut-brown with strong sinewy bodies. One had curly brown hair caught up on the top of her head in a messy clump, held up with what the Colonel suspected was an old paintbrush.

The other woman had interested him more. Her blonde hair was silvered with grey threads and she wore it parted in the middle and plaited into two plaits which hung down past her shoulders and rested on the top of her breasts. The Colonel thought she looked like a beautiful Native American Indian girl. It was as if she had stepped out of one of the romance novels that he read in secret in his garden shed. Instantly smitten. He had wanted to see her again. And that's why he came on the same day each week.

The Colonel slowly and carefully emptied the first bag of grass into the garden waste bin. Back at his car, bent over with his head in his boot he was just about to pick up the second bag when a woman's voice behind him asked.

"Do you need a hand with that?"

The Colonel's head came up sharply and connected with the boot-lid with a thwack and he ricocheted off and plunged face-first into the next bag of grass cuttings.

"Oh shit! Are you alright mate?"

The Colonel turned, his face covered in sticky green grass, looking like the proverbial Green Man.

"Bleugh!" the Colonel spat, spraying the woman with soggy grass cuttings in his efforts to speak. He rubbed the large egg-shaped lump forming on his head at the spot where his bald patch usually was, but which he had sprayed with theatrical hair dye before leaving the house this morning. This now sported pink patches due to the swelling and rubbing. "Oh er, yes, erm, definitely, I should say so, made of stern stuff, ha-ha, wasn't expecting, yes quite, thank you."

The Colonel was embarrassed and couldn't think of a thing to say, just stood there shuffling his feet like an adolescent schoolboy, when the woman smiled at him in an amused way.

"Come on let's get this stuff shifted shall we?" The woman grabbed a bag and pulled it roughly from the boot scattering grass cuttings over the pristine carpet adding to the ones the Colonel's head had dislodged, then headed off to the garden waste bin.

The Colonel looked down at his once pristine boot feeling distressed but just managed to stop himself complaining about her carelessness. Wanting to catch up with her he grabbed the next bag and trotted after her, admiring her tightly jean clad rear. After emptying the first two bags, they collected the last two bags disposing of the cuttings in the same way and the Colonel folded the garden bags up as they walked back to his car.

"Anything else you want shifted?" She asked as she peered in the car window.

"No, no, well just a few bits and bobs but I can manage those"

"No problem" she said opening the passenger door reaching in and grabbing Dottie's two carrier bags but as she straightened up one of the handles broke spilling the contents onto the ground.

The Colonel was mortified to see his wife's sludgy grey underwear and t-shirts spread out on the ground but was even more horrified when the last item fell out and landed perkily on top, a neon pink push-up bra!

The woman laughed as she bent to retrieve the clothes and bundled them back in the bag. "Wife having a clear out eh?"

"They're not my wife's!" spluttered the Colonel.

"Ooh, who's a naughty boy then" the woman teased giving him a cheeky wink.

"No they're my mother's!" Shot out of the Colonel's mouth before he'd had time to think it through.

"Wow you must have a nevrikos mama." At his confused look she said "feisty! Don't worry I'll deal with them." She strode off towards the clothes area, chuckling to herself.

The Colonel, frozen to the spot could only watch and admire her walking away swinging the bags at her side. His gaze slid again to her denim covered rear. She is perfect he thought, loving how her whole body fizzled with energy. The Colonel was aware of something beginning to stir down below. Embarrassed, the Colonel slid uncomfortably into the Bentley, pulling at the fabric of his trousers trying to ease them around his groin. But then he smiled, pleased that the Sergeant Major still had some life in him even if he wasn't quite up to full attention.

When it was time to take the next weeks grass cuttings to the recycling centre he was smugly armed with a little knowledge. First he deposited his garden waste then wandered over to the large assortment of cast-off items that had been sorted and arranged on various tables for re-sale. Although he appeared to be browsing with the intention to buy something, there was absolutely no way he would put any one of the disgusting items inside of his beloved Bentley.

His luck was in as an elderly lady pulled up in her blue Corsa and walked over to the container-office presumably to ask for assistance. Both of the recycling women came out and emptied the lady's boot for her. His woman (as he had come to think of her) to the Colonel's delight carried over a box of miscellaneous china and started to empty it onto the table next to him.

"Hiya" she smiled across at him.

"Hello, aren't you the young lady who is building her own house?" She must think I'm an idiot the Colonel thought. He couldn't understand why this woman turned him into a gibbering wreck, usually he was in complete control and accomplished at social occasions, so why was he blurting things out like a lovesick teenager?

"Yes, I'm building my second one now." She laid a rather hideous brown meat platter down.

"Your colleague said you're building it out of tyres."

"Yes I am, are you interested? Do you fancy having a go yourself? I'd have thought you would live in something a bit more traditional." She laughed to soften the comment.

"Gosh I wouldn't have the faintest idea how to go about it but I am interested." The Colonel replied.

"Well if you are interested there are tons of reasons why they are a good idea. For instance my house will remove 2,000 tyres from the planet. It's low maintenance and the solar windows keep the inside a constant temperature and that's just for starters. I could go on but I won't bore you."

The Colonel was mesmerized, he couldn't place her accent, it was definitely foreign and decidedly sexy. "You're amazing, I mean that's amazing, well done my dear."

"Right well gotta get on, nice talking to you, see you

again." With that she threw the box onto the floor, stamped it flat before picking it up and giving him a dazzling smile as she strode away.

"You OK buddy?" it was the other woman worker as she passed where the Colonel still stood starry-gazing.

Realising he was still staring after the woman, the Colonel gathered himself. "Yes, yes I'm fine thank you, must be off." I must find out her name he thought as he drove away. Since that first chat, the Colonel had seen her every week and in his besotted mind he thought that she made a point of looking out for him. They always spent at least ten minutes chatting and on the last visit she had even made him a cup of tea. He was so elated he hadn't even minded about the chipped mug or worried about how clean it was.

13
WHO SAID ROMANCE WAS DEAD?

The week following the sharing of tea, the Colonel visited a well known DIY store for the very first time. He hadn't wanted to use the local Ironmongers in the nearby town as questions may have been asked. It didn't start well as he tried to go in the 'Out' pushing several times before he realised everyone else was going in the other side. Once inside he hadn't a clue as to where to look and what to buy. After a few minutes he managed to stop an assistant.

"Where are the things you need to build a house?" he asked.

"You need to speak to Zephyr on building materials, I'm sorry I can't help you, I'm lights." And she whisked off before the he could ask her anything else. Where the hell do I find Zephyr thought the Colonel and what kind of imbecilic name was that? His father had had a Zephyr. Looking up he realised that there were large signs suspended from the ceiling indicating departments and he made his way over to Building Supplies.

He managed to locate Zephyr who was unloading a

pallet of plasterboard. Zephyr sported several tattoos, a large black ear expander and had hair shaved on one side and long on the other where it rose up and over his head mirroring Hokusai's 'Wave'.

Despite the Colonel's military bearing, background and disciplined outlook he was remarkably tolerant and serving in the army for most of his life he had learnt never to assume. Some of the quietest of men had proved to have a sadistic or cruel streak and some of the scariest and tough looking had been empathetic and caring.

So smiling at Zephyr he asked "I wonder if you can help me, a friend of mine is building an eco house and I want to buy a gift towards it. What could you suggest and it has to be something that would fit in my car?"

"Oh well that's interesting, what sort of eco-house is it? There's a few different types."

"I'm not sure. I'm afraid I haven't seen it but I do know it's made out of tyres."

"Sounds great. There are some things that every house needs. Let's have a wander and I'll have a think." Zephyr replied.

Zephyr wandered down the aisles with the Colonel following "This is very helpful of you."

"Guttering!"

"Guttering?" The Colonel looked at the three metre lengths that Zephyr stood next to.

"Probably too long for your car." Zephyr said. " I know! A rainwater butt, your mate will definitely be saving all the water he can. I've got a nice slim line model that he could use anywhere and it'll fit in your car." Zephyr showed the Colonel the slim green water-butt. "Even if they planned to use bigger ones around the house they could still use this on a greenhouse or shed."

"I think that's a great idea, thank you Zephyr, I really appreciate you taking the time to help me."

"I'll carry it up to the till for you."

Lifting it and tucking it under his arm as if it was as light as a watering-can Zephyr headed for the till, the Colonel in his wake. He dumped it down on the counter giving a cheery wave to the colonel as he headed off into the maze of aisles.

The butt just about went into the boot, thank goodness for that thought the Colonel. I certainly don't want it visible on the passenger seat and have to explain to Dottiewhy I've bought a brand new rainwater butt that I don't need. He couldn't wait to take it up to the recycling centre! It wasn't as if he was doing anything wrong exactly but he didn't think Dotty would understand. He wasn't sure if he understood himself why he'd bought it come to think about it. He knew he was acting completely out of character but couldn't seem to stop himself. He locked the car and went into the house.

14

DOTTIE

Dottie had never considered herself pretty and certainly not beautiful but she had thought she was reasonably attractive. Like her friends she expected to meet the man of her dreams, marry and have children. For reasons she couldn't fathom she was still single in her late thirties. All of her friends without exception had managed to meet 'The One'.

It was only chance that took her to the Colonel's house. He had made an appointment at the estate agents where she worked with one of her colleagues to value his mother's property for probate following her death. Unable to go due to illness Dottie had had to go instead.

She had never met anyone like him before. Most of the men she had dated only seemed to want one thing and if she fancied them then that was quite alright by her. Although some of them hadn't even managed to stay sober enough for sex. But as she had grown older she had wanted someone special of her own to make a home and have a family with. Her longest relationship had lasted almost six months but then the guy panicked and packed her in saying that he thought she was getting too serious. She'd given up trying to find a man who was looking for love and marriage as she was.

She had found the Colonel to be the perfect gentleman and when she had finished her valuation she stayed and enjoyed a cup of tea and some lively conversation. When she was leaving he had asked if he could see her again and perhaps take her out for dinner. She had put her business card in his hand and told him he could call her.

When the Colonel and Dottie had married, the Colonel insisted she didn't need to work and persuaded her that he wanted her to be there at home for him. Reluctantly she had given up the job she had loved. As an officer's wife she was expected to carry out a certain amount of pastoral care of the army wives but it wasn't really her cup of tea and she really missed her job, the people she had worked with and her clients.

They'd had a busy social life centred around the army and of course when he was away he wanted her to wait at home and be there to greet him on his return. It had been hard but she had always tried her best to be the typical supportive army wife.

Dottie had naturally assumed they would have a family but marrying later in life, (she had been thirty seven and the Colonel forty), time wasn't on their side. Roughly six months after the wedding the Colonel had moved into one of the other bedrooms. She didn't even know until it was time for bed. She'd gone up first and was reading when she heard the Colonel leave the bathroom. He came and stood at the bedroom door with his book and glasses in his hand and said "I'm not sleeping very well at the moment so I thought I'd sleep in the spare room for a bit." Without waiting for her to speak he had gone into the other bedroom and shut the door, leaving Dottie open-mouthed and confused.

That was when she looked across at the cabinet at his side of the bed. The top was empty of his clock and bits and pieces. Why hadn't she noticed when she first came to bed? She jumped out of bed and looked in his wardrobe, it was empty. Clearly this wasn't a temporary move. She climbed back into bed, hurt and confused. Admittedly their sex life hadn't been the best. She didn't think either of them had particularly enjoyed it and the Colonel had only managed to climax in the last couple of months. Dottie had always been left frustrated but was willing to put up with it now that the Colonel was performing, in the hopes that a baby might result from their uncomfortable couplings and that things would improve with more practise.

Before she'd married, she had enjoyed some rather delicious uncomplicated sex and was used to taking an active role. She had her suspicions that the Colonel had been a virgin when they'd married. Dottie, realising that the chances of having her own child were now gone forever was desperately upset and grieved for the baby she would never have.

She had raised the idea of adoption many times but the Colonel was adamant that he would not adopt. Not an unkind man but emotionally constrained, he wasn't aware of Dottie's sadness and couldn't empathise with her feelings of emptiness and unfulfillment. Dottie's desire for a child was overwhelming, she had so much pent-up love to give to a child and if she couldn't have her own then she wanted to adopt a child who needed a mother. Inevitably an invisible wall of resentment had built up between her and the Colonel of which he was completely oblivious.

When Dotties fortieth birthday was approaching she decided that when the Colonel went off on his next tour of duty, she would go away as well and blast her army pastoral duties. The cottage could be secured and left, they had no pets as the Colonel didn't like animals. This at last gave Dottie something to look forward to and to plan for. She didn't tell the Colonel, she thought it best to tell him after the event, she would be back home herself before he returned.

She decided on Greece, it was only a short flight away and she wanted to be somewhere warm. She loved the feel of the sun on her skin and being able to wear casual clothes instead of the more formal ones the Colonel favoured. About six weeks before they were both due to leave, Dottie pulled her small suitcase out from under the bed in the spare room, taking off the black plastic dustbin bag she used to protect it. Laying the case on top of the bed she unzipped it remembering the day she had bought it in an out of town shopping centre. She had known what sort of case she wanted, small, stylish, lightweight and with four wheels, so that she could manage it on her own.

The Colonel if he had been there would have wanted her to have a dark and boring one but she had bought the one she wanted. He could never understand why she wanted to go on holiday, he couldn't see the point when they lived in a lovely place. Of course he travelled with the army and didn't consider Dottie might like a change of scenery.

Before she'd married, Dottie had always loved the anticipation of a holiday and would always get her case out about six weeks before, popping things in right up and till the night before going when she would pack it properly. This secret holiday was no exception. The first items to go in were the most important ones, seven brand new pairs of knickers. She carefully laid them out flat, folded crotch to waist and then sides over crotch and then rolled them into a cylinder. Laying them tight together in a row, like toy soldiers in a box, She zipped up the case, covered it with the dustbin bag and slid it back under the bed. Over the next few weeks she continued to put things into the case and although the Colonel had no need to go into the small spare room, Dottie still made sure the case was hidden under the bed.

The day dawned for the Colonel's next tour of duty and Dottie drove him to the base from the cottage the Colonel had inherited from his mother. The Colonel never wanted her to park up and join the other wives doing the big farewell ritual, he preferred her to drop him off and return home. This suited Dottie and she waved and pulled away.

On this occasion driving home, although she still took pleasure in the beautiful Devon countryside, she was already anticipating her journey tomorrow. She parked in the drive and looked out at their traditional cob cottage. It was lovely but apart from a few minor changes and additions it was still very much the Colonel's mother's home. The furniture had been all of her mother-in-laws, the pictures, the knick-knacks, the carpets. The Colonel had insisted on no changes, he'd pointed out that everything was of a very good quality and heritage and there was absolutely no point in wasting money on replacing them.

Dottie had also pointed out that although she agreed with some of his points, it was only fair that she be able to make a few changes in order that the house felt more like theirs than his mother's. The Colonel finally agreed to move some of the pictures from the sitting room and they were put in the mostly unused dining room along with most of the knick-knacks. The collection of family silver stayed in it's display case, the walnut Bergere suite was moved into the newly built conservatory, which they'd both agreed on, as was the Aspidistra after negating the Colonels protest of "That Aspidistra has been in my family for years!"

"And it will do all the better for being in a hothouse environment!" She'd replied.

Lighter curtains, the wallpaper replaced with fresh emulsion a new comfy squishy sofa that the Colonel constantly complained gave him backache, new cushions and throws and the sitting room had been transformed. Still Dottie knew she could have walked away from it without a pang of regret.

Dottie opened a bottle of New Zealand Sauvignon Blanc, poured herself a generous glass and collected the ingredients for a simple supper. Bread, onions, garlic, pine-nuts, sundried tomatoes and olive oil. As she prepared the onions and garlic her thoughts travelled to Greece and it wasn't just the onions making her cry.

15

PINKY IN THE SHADOWS - STILL THE SAME SUNDAY

Celia left by the Cottles back door and walked around to the front of the cottage and down the path. She was thinking how strange that Dottie was already making plans to move away as soon as she could.

Opening the gate leading onto the road she heard a noise in the hedge and turning quickly, caught sight of Pinky Pope's face disappearing into the foliage. How odd Celia thought, Pinky was usually up for a chat. She closed the gate and turned to look up Pinky's path, catching a brief glimpse of him before his front door closed. She didn't go up the path but tried looking in Pinky's front window thinking to give him a wave but although she thought she could just make out a shadowy figure, he didn't come to the window.

This was very unusual behaviour from Pinky. Whenever she walked hirsute Roley past his garden, his pride and joy , he would call across to say hello and she'd have to cross over so that he could make a fuss of the little dog. He would roll over and throw his legs in the air for a belly rub. Hirsute Roley that is not Pinky! They would have a little chat about this and that, perhaps a bit of gossip. Celia would admire the wonderful flowers and vegetables and would often have a job to get away. He would never let her walk away without speaking. But not today. For some unknown reason Pinky was staying hidden, which was very peculiar thought Celia. Especially with all the goings on at the Cottles which surely Pinky couldn't have failed to miss.

That's not like Pinky either, thought Celia looking at the spade. It was partly stuffed business end first into a brown paper potato sack and lying close to the hedge. He would always clean his tools and hang them in his garden shed when he'd finished with them, he'd never leave them lying around in the garden.

16
PINKY POPE'S PINK VELOUR

Pink-Pope had gained his nickname at the ripe old age of seventy three after taking up running and setting his sights on the London marathon. This happily coincided with the annual WI jumble sale where he was delighted to find Mrs Bell's pink velour tracksuit at a bargain price of 50p! This was a double bonus for Mr Pope who had lusted after Mrs Bell since she was Trixie Tickler and sat in the row in front of him at school.

He hadn't stood a chance with Trixie. The closest he ever came was in a game of kiss-chase in the playground, when he'd caught her unawares and tried to grab her with his lips all puckered up and ready. She'd stamped on his foot and hit him over the head with her skipping rope. It was wooden and it hurt but even that hadn't deterred him. He'd spent most of his school years chasing after her but as she was the faster runner he never managed to catch her. But Dickie Bostock did. *And* she let him kiss her!

He'd always thought she'd looked down on him because his dad was a farm labourer and they'd lived in a tied cottage. Trixie always arrived at school neat and tidy in her beautifully hand knitted cardigans with matching buttons, pressed skirt and white ankle socks. His scruffy clothes were either oversized hand-me-downs from his brother or too small with the sleeves halfway up his arms and his shirt-tails refusing to talk to his short, short trousers. According to his mother he 'grew too quickly'; there was only a brief couple of weeks when everything fitted.

He wasn't alone in this, a lot of the other kids were dressed the same. Trixie of course was not. Her dad was a car salesman and her parents, as well as owning a car owned their own house. His mother said that Trixie's mother was no better than she ought to be (whatever that meant) and that she had no reason to look down on the rest of them.

Trixie was always turned out as smart as a bandbox, she would stay neat, clean and tidy, no matter what school activity she did. Even the day they all went to the river on a field trip and nearly everyone waded out through the water and mud to the little island and played about, Trixie stayed on the edge of the river in the shallows with her shiny black rubber boots, sparkling glass Kilner jar with a handle and brand new bamboo pole with a white net. Standing next to her was Dickie Bostock!

Dickie Bostock was his arch-rival, his dad was a carpenter! Not the kind that sorted your door out or mended a sash-window. Oh indeedy no, Dickie's dad made bespoke furniture for the rich and as Dickie boasted, for the famous! Of course he was ripe for teasing with his side-parting and national health glasses. "My name is Richard" he would shout stamping his foot at the same time, whilst the rest of the kids would shout Dickie, Dickie, Dick, Dick. Trixie was Dickie's friend.

Trixie grew into a beautiful teenager and Pinky would watch her play tennis at the village tennis courts. Tall and willowy with legs that went all the way up to Christmas, Trixie gave Pinky and the other lads many a wet dream through their adolescence. She went away to College and then to work in London where she lived with an aunt. She came back home to get married in the local church to her sweetheart Graham Bell ironically a telecoms engineer.

Pinky hadn't been invited but from his hiding place behind Alderman Headstone's headstone, he watched as the happy couple left the church. That was the last Pinky saw of her until, to Pinky's delight Trixie, now a widow herself had moved back to the village to care for her elderly mother.

Trixie Bell used to walk around the village three times every day as a way of keeping fit and she always wore a bright pink velour tracksuit. She was unaware that Pinky watched her from the safety of his sitting room, through his binoculars. He would have been horrified if people were to think it was in a stalking way but later on when Trixie Bell saw Pinky wearing her bright pink velour tracksuit she possibly thought differently.

Trixie's friends always knew when she was coming because her perfume would arrive a few minutes before her and then linger seemingly for hours after she had gone. Pinky never washed the velour suit, Trixie Bell's perfume wafting from it as he walked, gave him great pleasure. It wasn't long before some wag in the pub referred to Mr Pope as 'Pinky' and it had stuck.

Pinky and the Colonel had had a long running feud over their gardens ever since the Cottles had moved in, but things had finally come to a head at last year's Annual Village Show. Pinky had been winning the show cup for his flowers and vegetables for many years but since the Colonel had entered he had lost out in some of the classes.

Last year Pinky had grown the biggest marrow he had ever grown and he just knew it was a winner. When he had taken it to the parish hall on the day of the Annual Show, It was so big he'd had to move the other specimens over a bit to make room for it on the wooden trestle table. Sliding his name upside down underneath the marrow he stood back admiring it when the Colonel walked in and before laying down his own enormous marrow moved Pinky's out of the way.

Pinky was furious and picked up his own marrow. "How dare you touch my marrow!" Difficult as it was because of the weight he tried to wave it in the Colonel's face

"Call that a marrow, it's more of a courgette!" The Colonel sniggered and hefted his own marrow upright against the side of his chest as if it was a kalashnikov.

"How dare you, mine is bigger than yours!" Pinky said his face turning an unbecoming shade of red which clashed terribly with his pink velour track suit.

"I don't think so old man" the Colonel said, unwittingly calling him a name that to Pinky shrieked ageism and was like a red rag to a bull.

Pulling himself up to his full five feet, seven and a half inches Pinky spat back " I am not an old man! I am a vigorous middle-aged gentleman!"

"Well it's hard to tell in your pink pansy suit" was the Colonel's repost.

It seemed as if the Mexican stand-off would prevail

but Betty Bins who owned 'Bins Buns' in the main street and was Chairperson of the Autumn Show committee intervened.

"Gentleman! and I use that word reservedly. Remember where you are. You should be ashamed of yourselves, there are children and ladies present and I think you are *both* too old to get into an argument over whose is bigger than whose! Now pick up your marrows and leave the hall this instant. You have forfeited your right to enter." Betty turned her back on the two men and rearranged the other specimens.

Chastened they did as they were told and like naughty children slunk off to the front door of the hall where they both tried to exit at once, struggling to maintain hold of their huge Cucurbita Pepos. After a bit of rough jostling the Colonel being younger and stronger won the space and burst through with Pinky tumbling out after him. Many of the other villagers poured out of the door to see what would happen next, some definitely hoping for fisticuffs.

The Colonel stopped outside the door and turned to Pinky and said "It doesn't matter to me. I know I would have won first place with my marrow *and* the show cup."

Pinky stormed off, vowing "You won't win next year! I'll make sure you don't, one way or another if it's the last thing I do."

The protagonists lived next door to each other so they both had to walk the same way home. Pinky looked behind him and shooting daggers at the Colonel crossed the road. They walked parallel to each other but with Pinky having to execute a speedy half hop to keep up with the Colonel's march. This caused his marrow to jig up and down in an alarming manner as he held it in two hands, waist height.

Unfortunately at that precise moment Miss Lilac Davenport had just closed her front door and started to walk down her path. The sight of Pinky with his bouncing protrusion although fleeting, was enough to knock Miss Davenport off of her Lilac suede kitten heels. She was still sat there in a bed of geraniums when Monty Butler sauntered past. He didn't need asking once let alone twice to assist. Putting his hands down on the top of the gate he attempted to leap over, unfortunately the message didn't get to his feet and they stayed firmly on the ground. Monty had been dying to get his hands on the luscious Lilac and this was the perfect opportunity. Luckily Lilac was focussed on her footwear and hadn't noticed the failed athletic gesture.

Opening the gate in the normal way, Monty moved quickly down the drive and lifted Lilac off the ground where she had been sat mourning the broken heel of her shoe.

"What the fu...?" Started Lilac

"It's OK I've got yer luv." Reassured Monty.

"Well you can bloody well put me down! I've broken the heel of my shoe not my frigging leg!" Shouted Lilac.

Flustered Monty dropped Lilac heavily back down onto the already flattened geraniums and jigged about a bit on the spot like a naughty schoolboy. "Sorry luv, fought you woz in trouble like."

Lilac suddenly saw the funny side of the situation and looking up at Monty was further amused by his embarrassment. Not an unkind person she reassured him. "That's OK I appreciate your help."

But Monty was already reversing up the drive and

closing the gate behind him. Executing a quick wave he walked on.

Pinky was so upset and angry that that year was the first time ever he didn't go back to the Autumn Show ,not even for the prize giving later that afternoon, nor the auction of the produce later on in the evening.

17

SOLAR FLASH & SECOND THOUGHTS - EARLY AFTERNOON

The Inspector left the golf club sober and earlier than he usually would on a Sunday. Driving along, his mind was busy scrabbling around in cupboards looking for the thought that was tucked away somewhere in a dusty corner worrying him. Suddenly it came to him and swerving sharply he pulled over onto the side of the road and skidded to a halt. Much to the annoyance of a little old lady who had been following him in her black BMW and had to take action worthy of a presenter on Top Gear in order to avoid ramming into the back of him. Shocked and surprised the Inspector hadn't even realised anything was behind him. So engrossed in his thoughts there'd been no consideration for other road users in his wild manoeuvre. He put a hand up apologetically, as the elderly lady passed him, at the same time as she stuck her middle finger up with one hand whilst the other pressed on the hooter!

The giant solar flash that had just gone off in his head, concerned the Colonel's death. There was something that was not quite right about it and there was something. If only he could put his finger on it.. He thought over his visit to St Urith this morning and realised that he had been so annoyed at being dragged off the golf course spoiling his usual Sunday morning that he may have been a tad hasty.

Then he remembered a story his predecessor had told him about some meddling woman who had interfered with a previous investigation. He suddenly banged the steering wheel with the heel of his hand and shouted "What was that bloody woman doing there?" And she'd got there before him! It must be the same one. There can't be many women with the surname Ladygarden he smirked. God she must be able to sniff out a murder from a mile away!

Reaching across to the glove compartment he pulled out his notebook and pen. He was never without it, it was an invaluable tool and he just couldn't get the hang of writing notes on an Ipad, as some of the other officers were doing now. He started making a list.

1.Why did the Colonel stop mowing in the middle of a row?

2. Why was the Colonel lying on his back in the bath? If he had been washing the lawnmower surely he would have been leaning over the bath?

3. Why would an intelligent man try and clean an electrical appliance in the bath?

4. Why was the lawnmower plugged in?

5. Who would gain from the Colonel's death?

6. Speak to PCSO Boys

7. What state was the Colonel's marriage in?

The Inspector would probably not have been amused

to know that Celia also had a notebook about her person and that his list was almost identical to hers. Pulling out his phone he was not surprised to see he had no signal. There was no choice but to head on back to St Urith and the Cottles house.

18

SOME SERIOUS THINKING

Standing with her back to the cottage Celia looked across the green to the church opposite, deep in thought. Colonel Cottle's death seemed distinctly odd to Celia. It just didn't make any sense and if that bone-headed Inspector didn't think so, he had lived up to Celia's expectations.

And then there was Dottie? Although she was upset, she clearly wasn't the grieving widow! Who knew what sort of marriage the Cottles had enjoyed or not? They had been married for years and quite a chunk of that time the Colonel had been serving abroad. Dottie would have had to make a life for herself and been self-sufficient when on her own at home.

And what about Pinky? She turned and looked back at his house. His odd behaviour could be construed as suspicious and everybody knew there was no love lost between him and the Colonel. They had been at war ever since the Colonel had moved in and it was even worse after the fiasco with the marrows! She started walking letting the peace and tranquillity of the village soothe her.

19

RUMBLING TUMMY & EGGSPOSURE

Celia's tummy rumbled a distinct rumble, can't wait for my dinner she thought and turned towards home, walking around the green and towards the square at the back of the church. She thought of something to add to her list about the Colonel's death, which she hoped she would remember by the time she arrived home. She knew she should stop and write it down now in her notebook because these days thoughts seem to fly away on the breeze. She was always sure she would remember a certain something and then it was gone, it wasn't alzheimer's thank God, just age. Anyway she didn't want to stop, she was hungry and wanted to see Ronald and discuss with him what had happened at the Cottles.

Ronald had a way of looking at things from a different perspective and often noticed things that she hadn't, she needed his input. As she walked she was aware of twitching curtains, news spread like spilt milk in the village but bad news spread faster than the smell of dung on dung spreading day. Being very careful not to trip over the cobble path which sliced the square in two and was the old carriageway from the manor house, no longer there, she glanced at the clock on the church tower as she passed. It was just coming up to 5 O'clock, nearly time for a gin Celia was thinking increasing her pace at the thought, rounding the alleyway that led into her road.

"Arternoon me boody." Willy said as he stepped out in front of her.

"Oh good gracious Willy you made me jump, I didn't hear you coming." Celia replied breathlessly, her heart thumping behind her ribs.

"No one yers us a cummin me boody." Willy chortled away to himself "specially them courtin couples, they'm be gettin up to all sorts, if I told ee what I sees why eed mek ee air curl twould." Willy grinned his gap-toothed grin at Celia whilst enjoying a good scratch at his armpit; handily his shirt was ripped at the arm seam allowing access to the odorously irritated area.

"How are your chickens Willy?" Celia knew she had to change the subject or there was the distinct possibility Willy could teach her something she didn't want to know. She tried to focus on a spot over Willy's left shoulder but couldn't help herself watch in fascination as Willy undid the bailer twine holding his trousers up, hitched his trousers higher up his chest and then tied some sort of complicated knot all with his one and only arm. Unfortunately this only helped to highlight the distant cousin to the ripped seam in his armpit which was the ragged ripped seam exposing his groin!

Not to be diverted Willy went on "Oy zce this couple dreckly, ees stickin ees aid een 'n out the'm baint seed me...."

"I could do with half a dozen eggs Willy if you can spare them." Celia interrupted again desperately."

"You'm maids loikes it in't fresh air don ee? Oy mus tell ee bout"

"Well I must get on, don't forget my eggs Willy." Celia definitely didn't want to know what he was going to tell her 'bout' and made her escape. She turned back to the church and went down a side pathway taking the longer way home, now she was even more in need of a G and T. As she reached the bottom and was about to turn right she stopped and looked across at Dottie's cottage and out of the corner of her eye she saw a car turn into the road and pull up outside.

Should I or shouldn't I? Before she could change her mind she turned left and hurried back to Dottie's. She decided that she would walk down the front path and ring the front door bell, rather than going around the back to the kitchen door.

Willy was still standing in the same spot wondering where Celia had gone.

Chapter Twenty Two - An Inspector Calls...... Again - Same Afternoon

Celia wasn't sure who was the most surprised when the Inspector opened the door.

"I hope I'm not interrupting anything but I saw your car return and wondered if Dottie might need a friend."

"Come in Celia." Dottie called from the kitchen.

The Inspector had no choice but to stand back and let Celia in but he blocked her way in the hall before they reached the kitchen. " I have a few questions I need to ask

Mrs Cottle. Against my better judgement it might be a good idea for you to sit in on it."

"Sit in on it?" Queried Celia.

"I think you know what I mean Mrs Ladygarden." The Inspector's irritation could be heard in his voice.

"Is this a formal interview Inspector, because if it is I do believe that Mrs Cottle is entitled to some legal representation." Celia faced up to the Inspector not intimidated by either his attitude or his bulk.

The Inspector could feel his blood pressure rising but was determined that this bloody woman would not get a rise out of him. "This is just a quiet conversation and a few questions as I wasn't able to spend time with Mrs Cottle earlier due to a prior engagement." His eyes challenged Celia not to mention his earlier attire or indeed golf in any way.

Celia although tempted to comment on the Rupert Bear trouser ensemble decided this was an insignificant scuffle and one not worth trying to win. "I understand Inspector."

The Inspector turned and made his way into the kitchen with Celia on his heels. She went up to Dottie who was sitting at the kitchen table and put an arm around her shoulders. There was nothing she could say except the usual trite claptrap, like 'how are you feeling?' or 'are you OK?' which although understandable is absurd considering the circumstances. Who could feel fine or OK if you found your husband lying in the bath with a lawnmower on his chest electrocuted and to make it even worse he hadn't even finished the lawn. So instead Celia settled for the comforting arm and a little squeeze before sitting down next to Dottie.

There was a knock at the back door, the Inspector was

up and moving before Dottie could even speak. He had obviously been expecting it. The Inspector hustled in PCSO Boy who was dressed casually in jeans and a t-shirt and carrying a small shoulder bag. Closing the door behind him and giving Billy a disgusted look as he acknowledged the man- bag the Inspector said

"I thought it would be a good idea if PCSO Boy sat in and took some notes if that's alright with you Mrs Cottle? I asked him to come in civvies because I didn't want the neighbours to see and start gossiping."

"It's probably too late for that Inspector." As if on cue the telephone started ringing.

"That thing has been ringing non-stop all afternoon, I've left it to take messages and no I don't mind if Billy takes notes." Dottie smiled at Billy.

They all settled themselves down around the table and Billy pulled out a tablet from his bag and waited poised.

"What the hell do you think you're doing with that thing?" The Inspector asked.

"With the tablet I can take notes quickly, statements electronically, embed images, get people to sign with a fingerprint and I can do all this here immediately and....." Billy's enthusiastic explanation ground to a halt under the polar bear stare from the Inspector.

"You'd better know what you are doing with that thing young man, I'll want to see those notes on paper!" The Inspector started his questioning.

"Mrs Cottle?"

"Please Inspector call me Dottie."

"Right well ....Dottie, you can call me..... Inspector."

Celia had to pretend to search for something in her

bag to hide her amusement, eventually pulling out a tissue and dabbing her nose.

"Had your husband been depressed or upset about anything lately?"

"No, quite the opposite in fact, since he's retired he's taken more of an interest in the garden than ever before. He's always pruning and trimming things and the grass is cut till it's nearly bald. He's forever making trips to the dump. Then there's been the recent interest in the eco-build thing and he's been unusually jolly."

"Had he upset anybody lately or got any enemies?" The Inspector asked.

"Well to be honest the Colonel has upset a few people along the way, he doesn't....... didn't mean it, he was just a bit set in his ways but surprisingly he was also a very tolerant man. Why are you asking Inspector? You don't think somebody killed him?" Dottie's face paled at the possibility.

"You must admit Mrs C it was a bit of a strange way to pop your clogs!" Billy exclaimed.

"Thank you Billy, I think the Inspector can manage. You stick to your notes." Celia said sharply.

Billy quailed beneath the combined force of Celia's and the Inspectors admonitory gaze.

"Let's leave that for the moment, can we go through both you and your husband's movements from when you got out of bed this morning." The Inspector resumed his questioning.

"We both took our turn in the bathroom. I prepared breakfast as usual then the Colonel went into the dining room to read. As I said lately he's become interested in eco-building. He even ordered some books from the library and he's been studying them and making notes.

This is such a completely unusual interest for him and I'm still not sure if I can imagine him wanting to build his own house. Before all of this I would have been certain that he would *never* leave his mother's house!" There was an uncomfortable pause as they all realised what she had said.

"What did you do whilst the Colonel was in the dining room with his books?" Asked the Inspector.

"I was here in the kitchen preparing the vegetables for lunch, they're all still there in the saucepans." Dottie pointed across the kitchen.

"And after that?"

"We went to church to the 11.O'clock service together and afterwards I stayed behind to help with the teas and coffees and the Colonel went home to mow the lawns."

"Did anyone leave with the Colonel?"

"Well some of the congregation left, not everyone stops for refreshments but I couldn't say I remember who left at the same time as him."

"Dottie it's not a large congregation these days, did you notice if there was anybody new in church this morning, somebody that you hadn't seen before?" Celia asked.

"I was just about to ask that question!" the Inspector snapped giving Celia a look that would have shrivelled a coconut. "Remember you are only here as a friend."

"Well yes there was actually." Replied Dottie "but we do get new people from time to time, holidaymakers and the like. I do remember a woman slipped into the back pew just after the service started. The church door latch makes such an awful clunk as it's opened and closed, that nobody can sneak in or out without the whole congregation swivelling their heads for a good look. I didn't recognise her, she was youngish and casually dressed, other people must have seen her."

"Did you see her again after the service? Did she stay for refreshments?" Asked the Inspector.

"No, I didn't see her again, she must have left at the end of the service. We do get people from other parishes attending as well if there isn't a service in their own village that particular week. I certainly wouldn't know everyone, there are bound to be people I have never seen before. Why are you asking about strangers? Do you think a stranger did this?

Ignoring the question the Inspector asked "Dottie did you leave the church at any time either during the service or afterwards when you were helping with refreshments?"

"No I didn't leave during the service. Oh but I did run home for some milk during the refreshments, as we were running out."

"Dottie, I know you haven't had time yet to take it all in but you're an intelligent women. I'm sure you must realise the possibility that your husband was murdered." The Inspector held Dottie's gaze.

Into the uncomfortable silence, 'Enter the Gladiators' burst into the room. It was Celia's mobile phone. Scrabbling to find it in the specially designed pocket where it wasn't, she eventually found it in the side pocket where she kept her glasses. She answered the phone to an unusually voluble Ronald.

Celia could only pick out one or two words as they were galloping over each other in their rush to be said and they sort of merged together, probably as the result of one to many red wines with his lunch, she thought. But then she realised he was genuinely agitated and upset, trying to calm him down she told him.

"Ronald slow down and speak clearly." there was a pause "Oh my God, OK we'll be right there." Celia turned to the Inspector, her face white with shock. "Ronald was looking over the wall at the end of our garden and he says there's the body of a man in the churchyard."

"What! Another one? The body count is mounting up around you Mrs Ladygarden. Soon I'm going to have a policeman following you around in case of a sudden mortality. Boy make a call to Exeter for the SOCO boys, tell them to get here pronto. Mrs Cottle, I would like you to come down to the station for a formal interview tomorrow morning. I think there are a lot more questions that need answering. Don't leave the village and I will send a WPC to collect you at 9.30 am. Make sure you are ready for her."

Dottie had already concluded that it was a possibility the Colonel had been murdered. Especially because of the bizarre nature of the death But the idea was so outside of the normality of her life and so terrifying, she had thrust it quite firmly into a spare room in her mind and bolted the door. Hearing the Inspector use the word murder and startled at the tone in his voice when he told her that she would have to go to the police station for more questioning she suddenly realised the implications of what that meant. Panicked she looked at Celia for help. "Celia?"

"Dottie, this is just routine you don't have anything to worry about but if you have a family solicitor, you should ring him first thing and arrange to meet him at the police station."

"A solicitor! Do I really need one?" Dottie said becoming more distressed.

"It's only for your protection, it doesn't mean you're in trouble. I'm sorry to leave you like this Dottie but I have to go and see Ronald. I can pop back later or better still, why don't you put a few things in a bag and come and stay the night with us, you don't want to be here on your own."

"That's really kind of you Celia. I might just do that if you really mean it."

"Of course I do. I'll go home and get the bed made up and everything ready. Don't worry if it's late."

"OK thank you, but I'm not sure I'm going to be able to sleep tonight anyway."

"Come on Mrs Ladygarden I'll give you a lift in my car. Goodbye Mrs Cottle, I'll see you in the morning." The Inspector hustled Celia out of the back door of the kitchen, she just managed a quick wave to Dottie but she was anxious to get to Ronald.

Chapter Twenty Three - Dottie Alone

Dottie went to the Sitting room window to watch them go, the house was deathly quiet. Not for the first time she wished she'd had a dog. What was that? She heard a faint noise. It sounded like it came from the kitchen, immediately she tensed and her heart started racing. She told herself to stop being a wimp and pull herself together but although she tried, she couldn't move. That was definitely the back door and whoever it was hadn't knocked. Oh my God! Could it be the murderer coming back? She looked around for something to defend herself with, bugger, why had she moved all those nasty Knick-knacks to the dining room? She could do with a hefty china shepherdess figurine right at this minute but then she spotted the shiny brass model of Concorde, set on a mahogany base. That should do the trick.

She forced herself to move and crept across the carpet

The Curious Curiosity

picking up the heavy object and going back to hide behind the door. Holding the Concorde aloft it only needed a 'neeeoww' sound to make her look as if she was a child playing aeroplanes. Looking at the iconic sharp pointed nose of the plane, she realised that she was in danger of impaling a skull with it. She turned it around in her hands so that she was holding it like a brick, ready to bring it down on the intruder's head, forgetting that at five feet nothing most eleven year olds were taller than her!

She could sense the other person, then as they moved nearer she could hear their breathing. Oh God I don't know if I can do this, a scream rose in her throat...

"Dottie? Are you there?" a voice she recognised whispered.

"Nico?" she shouted in disbelief. How could he be here in her house and not in Greece.

"Yes it's me Nico. Where are you?"

She stepped out from behind the door and flung her arms up around Nico's head, forgetting that she had the heavyweight ornament in her hand. Nico dropped to the ground like a stone. Unconscious he fell backwards onto the parquet flooring, hitting his head with a thump, which only helped to increase the size of the lump already forming on the back of his head.

"Nico!" Dottie shouted again, kneeling beside him, terrified she had killed him. She tried to feel for his pulse but couldn't find it. Oh God! What had they said at that defibrillator training? Check his breathing that's it and if they're not then you do compressions on the chest to that BeeGees song, what was it? Oh God, shit, shit, what was it? Hang on what else did he say? That's it; if you feel able you can give the kiss of life, they'd practised on a dummy.

She carefully tipped Nico's head back and with one

hand pinched his nose and with the other opened his mouth, just as she remembered, then taking a deep breath she placed her mouth over his and almost immediately two strong arms wrapped around her and two firm lips kissed her open mouth and a warm tongue gently flicked inside. She was shocked, delighted and then angry pulling away yelling "You bloody idiot you frightened me half to death, haven't I had enough shocks today?" Then despite herself she flung herself back down on Nico's chest and hugged and cried in equal measure.

After she had cried herself to the embarrassing, red-eyed, snotty, hiccoughing stage, Nico pulled them both up giving her his handkerchief and then sat in the armchair pulling her onto his lap.

"Hey now, it's going to be alright." Said Nico.

"But Nico, what are you doing here?" Asked Dottie.

"I've come to take you back to Greece." Said Nico.

"But I thought you were waiting for me." Said Dottie.

"It was taking too long and I was worried that you would change your mind, so I came to make sure you would come back to me." Said Nico, tightening his arms around Dottie.

"Of course I am coming back but Nico, things have become a bit complicated." Dottie turned her head away.

" That is what I thought and this is why you are taking so long. I have been patient enough, so I have come here to make things right. Greek men are passionate and we do whatever it takes to get our women and I want you." He bent to kiss her again but Dottie stopped him and climbed off of his lap and slowly walked to the window.

Staring out of the window she didn't see the cows in the field or the Church standing solidly behind. Her mind was in turmoil. How long had Nico been here? She knew he was a passionate and loving man but did she really know him, after spending only a few weeks together? Did she really know what he was capable of? What if he'd done it? Was it possible? Could he have killed the Colonel?

Soft hands rested on her shoulders and Nico's hard lean body pressed closely to hers. He leant down and rested his face against hers saying softly "Dottie, what is it? I am sorry for frightening you but the back door was open. I know I should have let you know I was here in England."

How could she think such a despicable thing? This was *her* Nico a kind caring man, whose father was also a kind caring man. Of course he wouldn't have, couldn't have killed the Colonel.

"Nico, the Colonel is dead, I came home from Church this morning and found him."

"This morning! Oh my love, my poor darling, no wonder you are so distraught. What happened?"

"I don't know exactly, I found him dead in the bath." She couldn't bring herself to describe to Nico the scene she found in her bathroom this morning.

"But you mustn't feel guilty, it is not your fault. This is a cruel way your husband has been taken. He is making you pay for asking for the divorce. Please you mustn't let this affect us or our love for each other," he pleaded. "Now we are free to marry and have a life together."

"But of course it affects us! It's worse than you think Nico. The police don't think he killed himself, they believe he has been murdered!" Dottie couldn't help the sob that escaped. "And I think they suspect it might be me that killed him. I have to stay in my house until a police woman collects me in the morning to take me to the police station for questioning. As well as thinking I'm a murderer, they obviously don't trust me to turn up on my own. "

"Never! There is no way that you could kill anyone, this is probably a matter of routine. The police always suspect the husband or the wife in these situations. I will go with you in the morning and we must instruct a lawyer as well."

"Nico you can't go with me, they mustn't know about us and they mustn't know about you being here. If they find out about our relationship and that I wanted a divorce then we will both be suspects." Dottie suddenly felt faint and put her hand to her head as her vision started to blur and her legs started to give way.

"Put you head between your knees." Nico said as he helped her into a chair. "You've had a shock. Do you have any brandy?"

"Believe me you don't want to know, it's too complicated. Alcohol in this house is not as freely available as it is in the taverna. I think I'm alright now, let's go into the kitchen and you can make me a cup of tea, it's a panacea for all ills."

"You English and your tea." They made their way into the kitchen where Dottie sat down and rested her elbows on the table with her chin cupped in her hands." Pull down the blind Nico just in case somebody sees us and can you lock the back door as well please."

Nico did as asked and then filled the kettle up and started to look around for the tea makings. "Do you feel up to telling me what happened this morning?"

"OK." Dottie related the morning's events finishing with the telephone call from Ronald announcing that he had discovered a body in the churchyard.

Nico spun around "another murder? I don't believe it. Who was it?"

"I've no idea. This is normally such a quiet peaceful village, to have what might be two murders is quite incredible. I expect Celia will tell me what she knows when she rings later. Oh God I've just remembered, I said I would go and stay with them tonight."

"This is a friend of yours? Don't go to your friends I will stay here with you, no one needs to know. I will go back to the place I'm staying at to collect my things. I won't be long, will you be OK while I'm gone?"

Dottie wanted to show Nico the strong and independent person she used to be before her marriage, when she had been perfectly able to take care of herself. But today was different. She found that she liked the idea of Nico looking after her and certainly didn't relish the idea of staying in the house alone. Her feelings for him were so powerful that now he was here, she didn't want to let him go.

"Can I come with you?" Dottie asked quietly.

"Of course, a much better idea. Let's drink our tea and then if you are feeling better, I will go and fetch the car."

"No Nico It's still light we must wait until dark, we can't take a chance on anyone seeing us. I'm just hoping Pinky Pope next door didn't see you, he's usually in his front window keeping an eye on the goings on in the village. Where did you park your car?"

"Up the road near a war memorial, it's a hired car a dark blue Range Rover."

"When it's dusk you slip out and fetch the car, drive back past here and pull up just before the end of the road. I'm going to go through the back field and meet you there at the field gate." Dottie couldn't quite believe how devious she sounded. The Inspector had better not find out, as even she realised it looked suspicious.

"I am not ashamed of our relationship and we haven't done anything wrong. Do we really need to go to such lengths?" Nico asked.

"Nico please just trust me."

He put his arms around her and kissed her tenderly. "Everything will be fine my darling".

Chapter Twenty Four - Nico

Nico's life in New York seemed another world away as he sat in his first class seat on a flight home to Rhodes. It had all started with a telephone call in the middle of the night. Manos the village baker and his father's longtime friend rang to tell him of the sudden death of his mother.

It took him forty-eight hours from that call to touch down in Rhodes. There was the familiar rush of warm scented air that hits when you step out of the plane into a hotter climate, for Nico the scents of his homeland. It took another two hours to get to his home village of Lardon.

The taxi pulled up in the village square, next to the fountain that was fed from the river that ran down from the hills. He paid off the driver and stood taking in the sights and smells of his old home and although he felt deep seated grief at the death of his mother, his body relaxed.

Nico quietly opened the door of the taverna. Closing it behind him he walked across the dark room and reluctantly opened the door into his mother's kitchen nervous about what he would find. He was surprised to see that everything was clean, tidy and put away in it's rightful place. But then he should have known how it would be in his home village. This wasn't New York. The village women had clearly been in to help his father. Where was his father?

There was a loud thumping on the front door. Nico rushed to open it before whoever it was woke his father. It was Manolis, his father's friend. He told him that his father had been taken ill and collapsed. Manolis thought it was due to the shock of losing his wife so suddenly. He had been taken to the hospital in Rhodes. Manolis had been looking out for Nico and had stopped the taxi that was about to drive back to the airport. They both climbed in for the journey to Rhodes and the hospital. Nico trying to control his anger couldn't, help himself he had to ask the question.

"Manolis?"

"Yes Nico."

"Did you not think it might be a good idea to ring me and tell me my father was in the hospital in Rhodes before I left there?" Nico asked.

"Yes I did Nico." Said Manolis.

"But you *didn't* ring Manolis." Asserted Nico

"No, I didn't Nico." Agreed Manolis.

Nico tried to control his irritation because he respected this man, he was his father's friend and he was kind enough to come to the hospital with him. "*Why* didn't you ring Manolis?"

"I buy some cooking tins from my cousin Georgios friend's cousin's aunt's brother-in-law. They are bargain. Not to be missed. Non-stick. He has bakery like me, in the Old Town. So we can pick them up on the way to see your father, killing the two birds with the one stone. Not your father of course Nico, he is not a bird. Then on our return, I call in to my good friend Angelos. He send me message, he has some honey for me from his mother's cousin. It is the best."

Nico listening to this, knew there was no point arguing. He knew for sure that he was back in Greece. When you come from a small village like this, people like Manolis would always make the most of any situation regardless how sad the circumstances.

As they approached Rhodes town Nico grew more tense. Manolis had told him his dad was in the new hospital that hadn't existed when he'd left home all those years ago. Nico loved Rhodes old town with it's tall Venetian buildings, old churches and the Palace of the Grand Master. The street of the Knights undoubtedly was one of the best preserved Venetian towns in the whole of Europe. He promised himself a visit and a coffee at the picturesque port of Mandraki before he returned to New York.

In the hospital after asking at reception Nico was directed to the 4th floor and soon found the room he was looking for. Nico barely recognised his father lying in the hospital bed, hooked up to a bleeping machine. His once plump cheeks were sunken in, his skin looked clammy and grey and the aura of energy and joviality that had once surrounded him seemed to have disappeared. Nico had had no time to grieve for his mother and had been expecting to share his grief and mutual comfort with his father. But that had been cruelly snatched away from him and now he faced the prospect of losing him too.

As he entered a nurse was adjusting the thin cotton blanket around the silhouette of his father. She drew up the visitors chair close to the bed, touched him gently on the arm and with a small smile and a nod left the room.

Reaching through the metal guard he found his

father's hand. "Dad" he called softly wanting his father to know he was there. "Dad it's Nico, I'm here now dad." His father's eyelids flickered but didn't open.

"It's alright dad, you sleep, I'll be here." He felt the faintest of pressures from his dad's fingers and he seemed to relax and fall into a more restful sleep. After about half an hour there was a small knock on the door and the doctor arrived, she beckoned him out of the room. He didn't see his father open one eye and watch him walk away.

"Hello, I believe you are his son." She glanced down at her notes. "Nico?"

"Yes doctor, how is my father doing?"

"It may not look like it but he is doing well. The stroke has affected the left side of his face, his speech is affected and he has no strength in his left hand but doesn't seem to have suffered any other significant impairments."

"That's good news Doctor, will his speech and hand recover in time?"

Sometimes the damage is permanent but not always. The physio will see him tomorrow and give him a set of exercises to do at home. It's very possible he will recover some if not all the use of his hand. It was probably the shock of your mother's sudden death that triggered the stroke although it could have occurred at any time. But your father needs to change his lifestyle. He must stop his smoking, reduce his alcohol intake and take a little more exercise."

"You're hoping for a miracle then doctor. My mother and I have been trying to get him to do that for years."

"Unfortunately in my experience no matter what we say to a patient it is very difficult to persuade someone to give up if they don't want to. But let us look on the bright side. This episode may encourage your father to try. Your father's friend did well to get him to the hospital so quickly and although these machines look complicated we are only monitoring your father's vital signs and he will be taken off them tomorrow. Is there someone living at home to look after him when we discharge him?"

"Well I'll be staying for a while but I suppose I will have to get some help in the long-term?"

"I am sure he will do very well but as to whether he could or should run a busy taverna on his own I am doubtful. Why don't you go home and get some sleep, your father will probably sleep better now he knows you're here."

Nico took the doctor's advice and left the hospital but didn't go home. After sending Manolis on his way he booked into a small hotel nearby. It felt strange lying there listening to the sounds of Rhodes, so very different from the sounds of New York. He still needed to find out what had happened to his mother. What he couldn't understand was how she had fallen down the stairs in the middle of the day. She could find her way around the taverna in the dark. It just didn't make sense.

20

HAPPY RETURNS

Nico brought his father back to the taverna in a taxi. As they pulled into the square Nico was surprised to see at the taverna an attractive woman cleaning and setting out the tables for the day ahead. He didn't recognise her but that wasn't surprising considering his long absence from the village.

"You didn't tell me you already had someone helping you out dad, I was going to suggest that I help you find someone before I go back to New York." Nico said.

His father slumped on his arm "Nico, please don't mention going back yet, I am so tired and I don't feel well."

Nico immediately felt guilty, then angry for feeling guilty after all he was entitled to his life wasn't he? "It's OK dad, let's get you inside and I'll make you a nice cup of decaf coffee. "

"Cat's piss! I want a real coffee." His father said as they stepped up from the road and onto the terrace, which was covered with a roof of Mulberry branches, the trees standing sentinel around the edge.

The woman turned and came forward taking hold of Nico's father's hands and said "yassoo Georgios, ti-kanis?"

"Yassoo Dottie" his father answered, with his one good arm pulling her into an embrace and kissing her on both cheeks.

Nico was not surprised at the affectionate greeting this unknown woman had given his father. His dad was a practised flirt and raconteur who loved women and they tended to be flattered by his twinkling eyes, friendly bear-like appearance and genuine appreciation of the female of the species.

Georgios turned to his son. "This is Dottie our guest from England, she has become a dear friend. Dottie this is my errant son Nico who wastes his life working on those silly machines in a city the other side of the world; when he should be here helping me to run the taverna, marrying and giving me grandchildren. He broke his poor mother's heart."

"Thank you dad. Hello Dottie, very nice to meet you, don't listen to a word he says. My Mother was adamant I should spread my wings and see the world and she was very proud of my life and career; and so is this old donkey but you'll never hear it pass his lips."

Nico stared boldly at Dottie who had turned away from his dad shyly. Like many handsome men he was very aware of his own good looks and the effect he had on some women. Watching her pupils dilating and a softening in her face, oh yes he thought, she thinks I'm gorgeous. Then he found himself drawn to her unusually pale blue eyes. She tentatively put out a hand but instead of shaking it Nicos raised it to his lips and without breaking eye contact kissing it gently but firmly.

Georgios looked on amused, with a distinct twinkle in

his eye interrupted the moment by demanding coffee and a baklava and a sit down in his favourite chair at the end of the bar next to the entrance to the kitchen.

At first Nico was reluctant to let Dottie help around the taverna because she was a guest and on holiday. But having been away so long he wasn't as familiar with the day to day running of the business. Even when he had lived at home his mum had insisted he concentrated on his studies instead of working in the taverna. He had never been allowed to do any cooking because his mother had been queen of the kitchen. She had a young local girl she bossed around to prepare the vegetables but always did all the cooking herself; whilst his father had run the bar for drinks and coffees. Apparently even mastering the complicated coffee machine that was now installed behind the bar.

Nico observed that Dottie seemed to know her way around the taverna and was clearly enjoying herself. It irked him that she was more efficient at it than he was although he was pleased to note that she wasn't Miss Perfect. He loved watching her as she moved around and how she shed things as she went a tissue here, a bar towel there. He couldn't help but chuckle as he saw that the pink and white striped summer scarf that she had draped about her neck earlier, had somehow been caught and was hanging on the shoulder of Faustus the fishmonger; who had just absent mindedly tucked the end in his trousers as he endeavoured to relieve an itch in his groin.

Later, Nico's father, back in his beloved tavern, enjoying being feted by his old cronies and high on the euphoria of being alive; pulled out his white handkerchief and held it high in the air. He had to be physically restrained by Nico from joining in the Greek dancing. At the end of the night, Nico had helped his father into bed long after he should have gone but he'd been unable to prise him away from his friends and neighbours. Although tempted he'd stopped himself from interfering when he thought his father had had too much to drink. Why should he spoil his father's joy at being alive and amongst his friends. Tomorrow will be early enough to start him on a healthier diet and he certainly wasn't looking forward to being the one to enforce that.

Nico paused at the bottom of the stairs and watched Dottie as giggling, she pushed the last hardy drinkers out of the door and locked up. Then she picked up a tray, dropped a drying cloth and started to collect the the dirty glasses. The soft light from the lamp shone on her hair as she bent over the tables. The cotton of her shorts, strained slightly over her rounded bottom her brown legs smooth and bare. God what's the matter with me thought Nico, but there was something about this woman.

Suddenly aware, Dottie looked over her shoulder to find Nico staring at her. Instinctively she pulled down on the hem of her shorts, they were ideal to wear in the heat but not enough cover when you were faced with a Greek god. In fact she hadn't worn shorts in years but this holiday was all hers and she hadn't had to think whether the Colonel would approve or not. She had bought clothes she wanted but right at this moment she was wishing she was wearing an ankle length dress.

Nico crossed the room and took the tray from Dottie's hands and placed it on the bar "You've done enough work for one night. You're meant to be on your holiday, come with me, I think we deserve this." Picking up a bottle of red wine and two empty glasses in one hand he held out the other to Dottie.

Without conscious thought she placed her hand in his and followed as he pulled her through the back door and around the front of the taverna to a table on the terrace. There he lit the candle and poured them both a glass of wine.

They sat under the mulberry trees in the warm evening air and talked for hours until Nico could contain his yawns no longer. Dottie jumped up and said "I am so sorry, you must be exhausted and jet-lagged after all that travelling then visiting your father in the hospital. I think it's time we went to bed."

Nico's eyebrows rose questioningly a sly smile played about his lips that Dottie found very difficult to look away from."Really? And we've only just met." He said.

Dottie's gaze moved from his lips to his eyes as she suddenly realised what she'd said. "Oh my God, I didn't mean go to bed together that's unthinkable. Not that I think you're ugly or anything, coz you're not, you're gorgeous and any woman would be desperate to go to bed with you and Oh God! Shut up! Not you me. What am I saying? It's the wine, please forgive me." She stood up from the table and started to walk away.

Nico blew out the candle and followed her knowing that now it was pitch black she would struggle to find her way back. He called to her softly "Dottie wait it's OK, I was only teasing, give me your hand and we'll both go in."

Dottie nervously put out her hand and immediately Nico clasped it with his and led her back inside and across to the stairs. Turning her towards him he looked down at her. Dottie unable to stop herself looked up and unconsciously swayed a little towards him. Nico took this as a signal and leaned into Dottie pressing his length against her before kissing her, gently at first but as she responded, deeper...

By the time it came for Dottie to fly home, she and Nico were totally committed to each other. They had been sharing their lives and a bed for the past nine weeks. Dottie was returning to her old life but not for long. She had promised Nico that she would ask the Colonel for a divorce and as soon as she could she would return to Rhodes.

Nico was to fly back to New York so that he could sort out his affairs leaving him free to return to Rhodes. This time not for a visit but for good. His father had handed over the taverna to them and he and Dottie were determined to make a success of it, enough anyway to provide them with the necessities of life, bearing in mind the broken economy of Greece.

Standing amongst the noisy organised chaos that was Rhodes airport, Dottie and Nico were saying their goodbyes.

"Dottie I can't give you a ring yet but soon when you return to Rhodes we will choose one together. In the meantime as a symbol of my love I want you to have this. It belongs to my family and has been passed down the generations to me. It is sacred and unique, it will protect you and strengthen you in your resolve to end your marriage. It is the most precious thing in the Angelopoulos family. Do you love me and trust me enough to accept and believe what I say without opening it? And not to show or tell anybody about it and to keep it in the safest place in your home. I was going to say that it will remind you of me but perhaps not." he said with a huge grin.

Dottie looked at the small parcel Nico had handed to

her "I'm intrigued and a little nervous as to what it is but I do love you and I promise to look after it and bring it back. Nico I must go they have just called my flight, It won't set off the security alarms will it?"

"No it's pure gold tuck it inside your bra, next to your heart. "

They kissed tenderly and hugged fiercely then Dottie went through to departures.

On his plane travelling back to New York, Nico scrolled through the momentous changes in his life in the past few weeks. The loss of his mother he still hadn't come to terms with, he struggled to believe she had died falling down the stairs in her own home. When he returned to Lados he planned to find out all he could about her death. Before he had even arrived home following the news of his mother, his father had suffered a stroke and Nico agreed with the doctor that it was probably brought on by the death of his wife. He hadn't been able to add to his father's stress by questioning him about the circumstances surrounding her accident.

Then there was Dottie. If you had told him a few weeks ago that he would give up the successful life he had made for himself in New York for a woman he had only just met, he would have told you that you were mad! Could he really leave his comfortable Brownstone apartment on the Upper East Side where he enjoyed entertaining a large circle of friends. He knew he would miss his trips to the theatre, restaurants even the scruffy 6 train he travelled on to work. New York was fast-paced, exciting and probably the complete opposite of Lados.

He had enjoyed the company of various beautiful women but none he wanted to spend the rest of his life with. Until Dottie. Why had she got under his skin? She wasn't even free, she was married! Could he really give up the life he had built for himself over the last twenty odd years? The job that he loved?

Then he remembered the first time he'd seen Dottie. Her beautiful smile when she saw his father arrive back from the hospital and the obvious affection she had for him. It was a cliche but it felt as if he had known her for years. He loved how kind she was to everyone, always interested in what their customers had to say. Even old Papadopolous the fishmonger who if the odour didn't put you off, his monotone conversation about the joys of squid and grouper for hours would.

There were many things he loved about Dottie but most of all he loved that she was a real woman, there was no artifice about her. Most of the women he was used to were walking beauty counters. He'd come to loath the make-up stains and lipstick left on his shirts after an encounter. In the mornings if they had stayed over he would bring breakfast back to bed only to find them lying there in full make-up that had been reapplied in the time it took him to make some toast. Then they wouldn't eat it because they only ingested egg white foam for breakfast.

Dottie enjoyed her food and would laugh when the spicy sauce of a moussaka dribbled down her chin or the flaky filo pastry of a baklava floated down to settle onto her breasts. When he pulled her to the length of his body, she felt all woman with her soft curves and smell of soap and shampoo. When he woke in the morning he would watch her still sleeping until she seemed to sense his gaze and wakening would reach for him. With no thoughts of slapping make-up on. They connected in a way he had never felt before, he felt alive, invincible, loved. Reconnecting with his home through Dotties eyes he began to appreciate once more the quiet pace of life, the countryside around them and the joy of swimming in the stunning blue water of the mediterranean sea.

Life in Lardos would be busy in the summer when the tourists came but perhaps in the quiet of the winter months he would write that book. And he would be with Dottie and his father who he knew he couldn't abandon.

Nico's father had been overjoyed at their decision and was convinced it had all come about due to his matchmaking skills. Now he had time to sit in the sun playing backgammon with his old cronies and when the evening came he would move to his favourite seat, at the end of the bar near the door to the kitchen, so he could keep an eye on things.

21

HOME BUT NOT HOME

The plane was slowly descending into Bristol airport and Dottie was feeling apprehensive about returning to her life back in England. Rhodes was far behind her and seemed almost like a dream. Would she be strong enough to carry out the plans she and Nico had made? It had all seemed so possible when she was with Nico. He had made her strong and confident in herself, something she hadn't been for a long time. She wished that when she arrived home the Colonel would be gone, emigrated, anything but be there. How on earth was she going to be able to tell him! Strangely she hadn't felt any guilt when she had been with Nico in Greece but now back in England and reality, it washed over her. She just wished he would disappear!

Back home in the cottage she shared with her husband, the time she had spent with Nico seemed even more of a fairy tale. She put down her flight bag, sat on the bottom of the stairs and closed her eyes, conjuring up Nico's face and the feel of his arms around her holding her tight. Her love for him and the distance they were now apart overwhelmed her and she burst into tears.

22

RECYCLING CENTRE - BACK ALONG

"Where have you been? I know I said I would cover for you but I didn't think you'd be this long, it's been really busy!"

"Sorry Carol, had a bit of family business to take care of."

"I didn't think you had any family in England."

"Look! It's none of your business OK!"

"All right, all right, keep your hair on, only asking." Carol threw down an iron fire grate, narrowly missing the other womans foot and stomped off.

"Carol, I'm sorry, I shouldn't have snapped. Carol!" But her calls were ignored. She looked out over the hills so green compared to her own home.

23
QUEEN OF THE FORAGERS - SUNDAY AFTERNOON

Celia was anxious as she rode in the Inspector's car, when they pulled up outside her bungalow, she was out of the door and didn't stop when the Inspector yelled at her to wait.

Ronald had been looking out for her and had opened the door just as she reached it, they hugged each other tight. "You OK?" asked Celia.

"Yes I'm fine, it was a bit of a shock. I was only expecting to see a dead bird not a dead body." Ronald shuddered

The Inspector had caught up with Celia and said to Ronald "If you've contaminated the scene there'll be trouble!"

Celia affronted on Ronald's behalf said "Oh yes he probably climbed over the wall, tapped the body on the shoulder, looked in his half-eaten face and asked him if he wanted to pop over for coffee!"

"Good God! You didn't did you? And how do you know his face is half eaten?"

"Inspector why don't you .... go off (Celia

restrained herself, it probably wasn't a good idea to swear at the Inspector) up the garden while I make us all a cup of tea. You only have to lean over the wall a little as Ronald did to see for yourself."

Celia pushed in front of Ronald and made her way into the kitchen. She discovered her dear friend Veronica was there, sat on the bar stool at the end of the island. She looked like she had been through several hedges backwards. Her blonde mid-length hair was fluffed out around her head like a startled cockatoo and decorated with the odd leaf and twig. Her favourite dark green sweatshirt with the large duck motif was covered in bits of old moss and unknown organics. The multitude of pockets in her camouflage trousers were bulging with the results of her foraging and Celia shuddered at the thought of what might be wriggling around in them. In her hand was a very nearly empty glass of wine and on the worktop a very nearly empty bottle of wine. At her feet lay her large canvas shoulder bag bulging at the seams. What delightful delicacies has she brought us now thought Celia, knowing It was probably stuffed full of unusual and often distinctly unpleasant things.

Veronica was a serious forager. Unfortunately she also had a generous and kind nature and would insist on sharing whatever she had found. It was always a pleasure when she popped in looking to share the odd tipple or two, but Ronald and Celia were definitely averse to drinking her home brew concoctions. The last one she brought was infused from pine nuts and dandelion leaves. Apart from the fact that when they eventually woke up the next morning with badgers breath and a combine harvester working in their heads, neither of them remembered her even leaving the night before. Everything they ate for the next three days tasted bitter and metallic, even her porridge which Celia had put extra honey on!

"This is all a bit Giant Hogweed, isn't it dear" Veronica downed the last of her wine and reached for the bottle."

Celia just managed to get there first and holding onto the bottle with one hand she took out a fresh glass from the cupboard and poured herself the last of the wine. Ronald began explaining to the Inspector how he had discovered the body.

" Well, Veronica brought us her latest alcoholic beverage made from foraged fruit but I had to siphon the liquor out from the kilner jar..."

"It's called Diodgriafel made from rowanberrys, it's a very old Welsh recipe, found it in an old book up the dump." Veronica interrupted enthusiastically

"Can we get on?" The Inspector snapped.

"Okay keep your hair on." Ronald said unaware that this was a sensitive subject with the Inspector as every morning he was having to inexpertly comb over the balding patch on his crown. He instinctively put his hand up to the patch of pink hoping it was still covered.

Celia managed to conceal her smile but Ronald completely unaware of the Inspector's reaction continued with his story.

"I was looking in my shed for a piece of tubing to siphon out the liquor but couldn't find any, then I had a thought...."

There was a loud sigh from the Inspector.

Ronald gave him a look which said, 'I'll say it in my own time' then continued,.

"The washing line! Perfect, so I walked up the garden path to the concrete post that the line is tied around because I knew there was some extra line that was wound around a hook. I pulled a length off and then realised I'd left my knife in the shed..."

"Please Mr Ladygarden, get to the point!"

"Just let him get there in his own time inspector, I usually find it's the only way." said Celia.

"Well I was pulling out the string from the middle of the tubing......"

A groan came from the direction of the Inspector but Ronald carried gamely on.

"I'd just got the string out and the piece of plastic tubing was just perfect for syphoning when Veronica came out to see how I was getting on."

"That's right." Said Veronica. "And hirsute Roley came with me, he darted up to the end of the path and I thought he was running to Ronald"

"But he shot past me and was jumping up against the churchyard wall barking."

"Ronald said it was probably a cat but me being nosy, I leant on top of the wall for a look and that's when I saw it, him." Veronica turned a little pale "It made me quite faint, I had to have a little drink to revive me."

"Or two or three" muttered Celia.

"Right I want you all to stay here in the kitchen, that includes you Celia. When the SOCO boys arrive, send them out."

Celia and Ronald stood at the french windows and watched as the Inspector walked up the garden towards the churchyard wall. Veronica losing interest had gone into the kitchen, emerging with a full bottle of wine. She sat on the sofa where she poured herself another glass.

Celia was itching to get out there and look for herself but just then the doorbell rang, it was the SOCO 'boys' as the Inspector called them. Who were to Celia's delight all women apart from one man, who was *not* in charge. She showed them through the house, then led them out into the garden to where the Inspector stood looking over the wall, an old fashioned handkerchief pressed to his nose. Celia warmed to him a little as she firmly believed in cotton handkerchiefs. Whilst he was involved with the SOCO team, Celia took the opportunity of having a ganze over the wall. It wasn't as gruesome as she had thought except where the face had been chewed was a bit unnerving. She quickly scanned the body but there were no visible signs of death, no knife sticking out or a bloody hole from a gunshot. She'd just spotted something on the wall next to the body and she was trying to decipher the letters when a manly hand gripped her just above the elbow and steered her around.

"Celia, why don't you go and see if you can rustle up some tea for the boys." The Inspector said

One of the SOCO women looked at her and winked.

"Yes of course Inspector, no problem." Celia turned and walked back down the path stopping beside the boundary fence. As she stood there on the path, the fragrance of her roses wafting around her, she started shuffling the pieces of the puzzle around in her head. Why was the Colonel interested in eco building? It was completely out of character according to Dottie. Why was Dottie acting so strangely for a newly bereaved woman? What was the significance of the Greek postcard? Then there was the man lying dead in the Churchyard and what was the meaning of the letters scrawled on the wall? Someone had tried to rub them out but she had been able read some of them, SNOT and then possibly two blurred letters.

Her thoughts were running around in her head like

ball bearings in a 'Mousetrap' game. Knowing she needed to calm her thoughts and gain some insight into what had been happening, she practised mindfulness. She dropped her shoulders which she was wearing up around her ears like a scarf and gazed into the distance.

The beauty of the Devon countryside never ceased to lift her spirits, it was like watching end to end episodes of Countryfile, always something going on, always changing. She could see on the far hill a tractor marching up and down the rows turning the silage over, taking advantage of the warm dry day. They would work on many fields through the night. It would all be picked up, rolled, wrapped in plastic and stored away until the winter when it would provide nutritious food for the animals.

Between two stands of trees on the horizon she could see the hills of Dartmoor. Just across the next field the sheep with their lambs, who formed small gangs, playing chase around the telegraph pole and running the 100 yard dash. Their happy bleats mixed with the watery chomping of the cows in the field next to the house. As usual when anything was happening in Celia's garden they were hanging their heads over the fence. They were so nosy, they especially liked music. When Celia or Ronald were watering the garden, they absolutely revelled in being sprayed with the cold fresh water, curling and rolling their huge fat tongues to catch every drop.

With her mind relaxed, a memory freed itself from it's hiding place on the seabed of her mind and floated into her sea of consciousness. A few weeks ago a stranger had been seen in and around the village throughout the day. That same night he had scared the nightlights out of Tommy Alcock who was on his way home from the sports club where he had been playing snooker with his best pal and rival Eric Beech. Could this be the same man mused Celia? Deciding that she was a few pieces of the puzzle still missing and that she needed to get some more information out of the Inspector especially about the dead man, she went in to make the tea.

Celia had brewed a large pot and was just getting out the mugs when the phone rang, asking Veronica to answer it, she carried on.

"The Ladygarden residence, fabulous forager Veronica speaking. Oh, right yes, I'll tell him or I'll tell Celia my friend and super-sleuth. Shall I send her instead, she's very good? Well really, Rude!"

"Veronica! who was that?" Celia asked "You can't go around putting the phone down on people!"

Veronica walked to the back door "I didn't, she put the phone down on me! Anyway it wasn't for you it was a message for the Inspector, I'll go and tell him." She had gone before Celia could ask what the message was. She walked back in the door a few minutes later just as the phone rang again. Celia stopped pouring and slammed the teapot down as she moved to answer the phone but Veronica got there first.

"The Ladygarden residence, fabulous forager Veronica speaking. Sorry you're speaking too fast, I can't understand you. Hold on a sec." She muffled the phone against her body. "Celia it's a female hysterical shall I cut her off?"

"No wait, give it to me!" Celia reached for the phone as Veronica tottered towards her.

"Hello? Celia here. Trixie? Is that you? What? Oh my God not again. OK, don't worry Trixie. Go into another room and I'll be there as quickly as I can. Veronica can you take the tea out to the Inspector's people. Without the

Inspector hearing can you tell Ronald quietly, I've had to pop out for a minute."

"OK but it will be difficult."

"Why?"

"You know why. Ronald will never hear me if I say it quietly, so he'll ask me to say it again, then I'll say it again and then he'll tell me to speak up coz he can't hear me and I will and then everyone will hear me, including the Inspector!"

"What's that about the inspector?" Asked the Inspector as he came into the kitchen.

"Nothing." Said Celia in as casual a manner as she could manage given the circumstances of desperately needing to go in response to Trixie's distraught phone call but not letting the Inspector know because if he did he wouldn't allow it.

"Celia, I have just had a message that I need to go to Stragglers Bottom, I think you ought to come with me."

Celia looked at the Inspector in surprise, "Really?"

"Yes. I don't think I have ever had to say this before in my career but we have found a third body." The inspector said.

"How did you know Pinky was dead?" Celia asked.

"Your friend Veronica just gave me the message from the station. And how did you know Pinky erm Mr Pope was dead?"

"Trixie phoned me."Celia gave Veronica one of her looks, "Really Veronica?" then shaking her head followed the Inspector out, calling over her shoulder, "Don't forget to tell Ronald where I've gone"

24

PINKY FINALLY GETS TRIXIE'S ATTENTION

The Inspector pulled up outside Pinky's house "I can't believe it's called 'Stragglers Bottom' and I definitely don't want to know why!"

"Pinky named it after his beloved granny's house, it was called that because it lay at the bottom of a valley. Pinky had happy memories of visiting her. Why Inspector, whatever were you thinking?" Celia asked innocently.

Slightly red in the face the inspector answered "I'm not sure what's going on here Celia, we appear to have a serial killer on the loose but I don't think it's random. Apart from the man in the churchyard, two of the victims are people in the same village. They must be connected in some way. I'm betting that we'll find Mr Pope has been murdered too and he lives right next door to the Colonel. There's no such thing as coincidence when it comes down to murder. I want to catch this bastard before he kills again and before the big boys from Exeter get wind of it, they would have been crawling all over us by now if it wasn't a Sunday! I only got the S.O.C.O team here because they were hosting a stand at an employment fair in Ilfracombe.

The Inspector paused and when Celia turned to look at him, he said. "Celia, I know we've had our differences but you live in this village, you know these people and I would really appreciate your help."

Surprised, Celia replied "I'll do anything I can Inspector. Like you I believe that these murders are connected but at the moment there are too many missing pieces to complete the puzzle."

"Just make sure that you share any information you discover or insights you might have, however vague. This is police business not a game you know."

Biting her tongue lest she tell the Inspector where he could shove his patronising attitude, she just grunted a response and went to step out of the car when suddenly Willie appeared from nowhere. Unfortunately Celia had already swung her legs out and found herself face to groin with the unsavoury chap.

"Willie! you frightened the life out of me!"

"Alright me andsome? I wus a bringin yer eggs and then I seed ee. Wher be goin to me dear? Spector you'm wanna find they ol vurriner I seed ee creepin round, med me savage. I reckon ee be wun' o they sylem seekers affer my ens. Well e baint gonna ave em. Fred down at Unkempt Muff zes they'm after our jobs and wummin ave ta be a wearing that they burky and pray ever day and I only go church arvest fer me coupla tins of tomaty soup and Christmas time fer the mince pies, andsome they is."

"Willie!"

The poor old chap jumped at Celia's shout.

"Sorry Willie I didn't mean to shout at you, I am a bit fraught. But firstly you mustn't go around saying nasty things about people you don't know. Secondly the pub is called the Unfurled Moth. Thirdly you and Fred are already a couple of idiots. Thank you for the eggs, now I suggest you go home before the Inspector decides he wants to question you." Celia told him.

Willie taken aback at Celia's onslaught and the threat of questioning by the Inspector, thrust the eggs in her hand and turned tail for home.

"So it's possible Willie's foreign gentleman and the body in the churchyard are one and the same. Let's hope the SOCOS turn up something that will help us identify him" The inspector said.

They knocked on Pinky's front door and after a few moments it was opened by Trixie Bell.

"Oh Celia. Poor Archie, I think he must have had a stroke, I knew he was dead I checked his pulse and held my handbag mirror against his mouth to check for breathing. There seemed no point in calling for an ambulance and then with all the goings-on in the village I thought I should call the police, so I phoned Audrey Boy and then I thought you would know what to do with all your experience."

"Audrey Boy is not the police and you shouldn't have touched the body madam, you have probably ruined the crime scene!" The Inspector snapped at Trixie.

Not intimidated at all by the Inspector, Trixie shot back. "Audrey's son is a policeman and I am not psychic Inspector, how did I know it was a crime scene? I did what any sensible person would do when coming upon an unconscious person. We did the training when the defibrillator came to the village didn't we Celia? Although I must admit to feeling that something was not quite right before I had even checked poor Archie."

What was it that made you feel like that Trixie? Can you remember?" Celia asked.

"Well I think it was the stillness, as if there was nothing or no one in the house to disturb the air. You know sometimes you can just tell if there is someone in a house or not." Trixie explained.

"What made you come here Trixie? I didn't think you and Pinky I mean Archie were friends." Celia asked

"Oh I knew all about Archie's feelings for me, he's been in love with me since we were at school together, just because I didn't have any romantic feelings for him, didn't mean I didn't care." Replied Trixie.

The Inspector looked at Trixie and saw a woman in her late sixties, with short suspiciously brown curly hair, sparkling eyes and a smiling mouth. She wore a pair of grey jogging trousers and matching zip-up hoodie jacket over a bright pink t-shirt revealing her plump figure. Still an attractive woman, he could imagine her as a pretty young schoolgirl and understood why Pinky had been fond of her.

Out of his pocket the Inspector pulled some blue plastic shoe protectors and gave a pair to Celia. "You can come in but I want you to just stand inside the door against the wall, far enough in the room so that you can get a good look around but no further. Understood?"

Celia pulled on the plastic covers and said "Understood."

Going first the Inspector stepped into the sitting-room and sidled around the wall with Celia following behind. Looking around the room everything looked neat and tidy as if nothing had been disturbed.

"His neck looks a bit odd." said Celia looking at the

back of the armchair with Pinky's head and neck just visible.

"Mmn probably broken but it doesn't look as if there was a struggle, so the murderer came from behind. Hang on" The Inspector stuck his head out of the door and called. "Mrs Bell! Would you mind coming back in here for a minute. He waited until Trixie stood in the doorway. I'm sorry to ask you but Is everything in here exactly as you found it?"

"Yes Inspector, I didn't touch anything except Archie. " Said Mrs Bell, dabbing her eyes with a tissue she had pulled out of her sleeve.

"Right, thank you." The inspector started to turn but stopped and asked "Mrs Bell was the television on when you arrived?"

"Yes I turned it off, Archie always had it on so loud because he was a bit deaf. Sorry Inspector I didn't think." Mrs Bell answered.

"Don't worry Mrs Bell, it's fine I just needed to know." The inspector came back into the room and said to Celia "He probably didn't hear a thing."

"But why kill Pinky, he was a harmless old chap." Celia looked down at the diminished figure of Pinky almost swallowed up by the large armchair.

"That's what we need to find out Celia."

"He must have seen or heard something this morning at the Colonel's." Celia said. "But why didn't he tell the police, *unless,* he didn't know that he'd seen something but the killer thought he had. He was acting very strangely when I saw him this morning."

"You didn't say you had seen him this morning. Where? When?" Demanded the Inspector.

"Well I didn't think it was important until now. Why would I? I did think it a little out of the norm though. Pinky liked to.... Used to like to talk to everyone who passed by his cottage, he was a bit of a Nosy Parker and barring a hurricane or snowstorm would usually be working in his front garden. It has been lovely all day today and yet when I left Dottie's cottage earlier, although I caught a glimpse of Pinky through the hedge, he shot indoors before I could speak to him; almost as if he was avoiding me." Celia said.

"Until now Archie Pope was on my list of suspects. PCSO Boy told me he had been in some sort of garden war with the Colonel for years and he'd been seen making threats to the Colonel." Said the inspector.

"As I say I did think Pinky was acting strangely earlier. I'm sure he must have seen me because I caught a glimpse of *him* before he shot inside and again through the window but he stepped backwards into the shadows." Celia said.

There was the sound of voices from the kitchen, then PCSO Boy appeared in the doorway.

"Sir?" Billy saw Pinky in the armchair and visibly paled and slumped a little sideways against the doorframe.

"I'm afraid Mr Pope has been murdered Boy. Take a moment to collect yourself, I expect this is a bit of a shock to you. You've probably known him all of your life and this has been a long and trying day." The Inspector said not unkindly.

"What's happening sir? This has always been a quiet friendly village, this sort of thing just doesn't happen in St Urith."

Celia knew that the best thing for Billy was to give him something to do, so she asked him.

"Billy would you go into the kitchen and look after Trixie? She found Pinky and is rather shaken up. Perhaps you could make her a cup of tea." Billy nodded and went off to the kitchen.

The Inspector indicated to Celia that they should leave the room and they both walked through the hall and out of the front door.

25

CELIA & THE INSPECTOR IN CONFLAB

"We'll have to wait for the SOCOS to finish in the churchyard, let's hope they find something that will help us; they shouldn't much longer." Said the Inspector.

"Inspector If we leave Willie's furriner out of things for a moment, what have we left? It seems to me that everything focuses on the Colonel's house, even Pinky's murder."

The Inspector looked out across the green towards the church. " It's such a peaceful scene, hard to believe what's happened here today. OK Celia against my better judgement I'm going to have to give in and use your knowledge of the village and the people in it. So what have we got?

The Colonel was murdered by person or persons unknown in his own house."

"The house had been partially searched but it was carefully done, it wasn't trashed. Isn't that a bit unusual?" asked Celia.

"Yes, burglars don't generally worry about making a mess, they're in a hurry. Unless it's the sort who deliberately cause as much damage as they can and that's definitely not the case here." Responded the Inspector. "I think someone was looking for something."

Celia looked at the Inspector with a newfound respect. "Well this person must have been watching the house for some time to know the Cottle's routine. They were in a hurry because they knew they only had a short time until Dottie came back from church." Said Celia

"Unless....it was Dottie who murdered her husband and she moved a few things around to make it look like a burglary gone wrong."The Inspector said.

"But inspector, don't you think it was rather an elaborate and bizarre way to kill someone? If you wanted to kill your husband I can think of far simpler methods. This murder is so out of the ordinary, despite you initially thinking it was an accident which by the way is nearly as bizarre. Could it be that the person who did this is trying to frame Dottie?"

"Celia, I know you don't want to believe it but Dottie is the most likely suspect and I think you must agree with me that she is not your typical grieving widow." The inspector said.

"I do agree that she doesn't seem as distraught as one would expect but perhaps their marriage wasn't a particularly happy one. I think the Colonel must have been a bit of a control freak and possibly OCD. It seems as if they led fairly independent lives. That's understandable when they were apart for such long periods." Celia said.

"There's something not quite right about her, she's keeping something back and I intend to find out what it is when I interview her at the station in the morning."

"You could be right inspector. But if Dottie's not the murderer I'm worried about her safety tonight. The killer is still out there and that's why I asked her to come and stay. I've been thinking about it and I'm convinced there is something in that house someone wants very badly and they will stop at nothing to get it."

"That's a bit dramatic Celia, I think you've been reading too many murder mysteries. But I do think it's a good idea she stays at your house tonight and I am going to put PCSO Boy on watch outside her house."

"Poor Billy, he'll be exhausted after all the trauma of the day."

"Big learning curve for the boy but don't worry about him. I'll get a couple of hours sleep and then if reinforcements don't arrive I intend to take over from him later in the night."

The SOCO's pulled up in their van ready to process the murder scene at Pinky's. The Inspector walked back into Pinky's and told Trixie that a WPC would pick her up in the morning along with Dottie and bring them both to the station for a statement. Then he turned to Billy.

"PCSO Boy I want you to walk Mrs Bell home and then I want you to come back here and keep watch at the Cottles and the Pope house. Make a note of anything suspicious or out of the ordinary. If anybody attempts to enter either of the properties, ring me immediately ."

The Inspector dropped Celia off at home. "Celia. See you get a good night's sleep but if you think of anything or if Dottie discloses something to you tonight you must telephone me straight away. Agreed?"

Celia hesitated then answered "agreed."

As the Inspector closed the garden gate he looked sternly at Celia and said "Whatever you do, no snooping on your own. As you said yourself there's a killer on the loose and it's not worth taking chances with your life." He turned, got into his car and drove away.

Celia watched his taillights disappear down the road before going in, closing the door and locking it behind her.

26

TEA AND BUNS - SUNDAY EVENING

PCSO Boy on stakeout as instructed by the Inspector unfortunately didn't notice Nico, who had slipped out of Dottie's back door and climbed over the fence into the field at the back of the house. Nico had carefully walked down to the gate on the corner and climbed back into the road, past the stakeout car towards his parked just up the road.

The reason for Billy's inattention had been the arrival of Dusty with tea and buns. Billy had a serious crush on Dusty and the pair had been dilly-dallying around each other for the past twelve months. All they had managed so far was the occasional hello when passing in the street or meeting at various village dos. Billy hadn't the courage to ask her out but in the last month he had managed to friend request her on Facebook.

Naturally the whole village knew about Billy's stakeout. Betty Bins had instructed her daughter to "Take the poor boy some refreshments."

So when Dusty climbed into Billy's mother's Corsa

with a flask of tea and mum's buns, it constituted a first date!

Dusty's mother ran her own bakery 'Betty Bins Buns & Batch' she only made two products, rock buns and batch loaves, using recipes passed down in the family.

"If it was good enough for my dad and my granny before him it's good enough for me." She would say if anyone dare suggest she might like to expand her repertoire. Unbeknownst to all but a few close friends, Betty did in fact make Bun Gin using golden sultanas. According to Betty's forebears it was made for medicinal purposes particularly for arthritis. Betty's rule was that you drank it to prevent arthritis and you drank it to relieve the symptoms of arthritis.

Betty and Dusty lived in a lovely roomy flat above the Baker's shop with Betty's mother Ruby, her father having died when she was young. Ruby spent most of her time sitting in her special chair in the big bay windows that looked out over the Village green. She would sit and knit, keeping an eye on her neighbours comings and goings.

When Betty's dad the baker died when she was ten, her mother Ruby cut off the long hair that he used to love, rolled up her sleeves and ran the bakery single handedly. Betty always loved living above the bakery. She would lie in bed with the smell of fresh baked bread seeping up through the cracks in the oak floorboards, filling her bedroom, making her mouth water and her tummy rumble.

In her mind's eye Betty could see her father, sweat dripping off his brow, the sleeves of his flannel shirt rolled up, muscles tensing as he pulled out the hot heavy trays of batch bread. When the bread was cool her mum would split them up and put them on the shelves in the shop.

With her dad gone she had to help her mum in the bakery and she especially enjoyed baking the buns. That's when she had made up her mind to work there when she was old enough.

By the time she'd finished catering college Betty felt differently, she felt restless and trapped in the bakery and the small village. Flying in the face of her mother's flat refusal she had gone travelling to find herself. Whether she had found herself or not, she found something, because she returned home eighteen months later, eight and a half months pregnant. Accomplishing her mother's worst fear.

Ruby welcomed Betty back with love and compassion. Not one question asked or one word of recrimination spoken. Betty was swept up in a swirl of activity because there was little time to prepare before the baby came.

Together they had cleared out the little box room next to Betty's, decorated it with pale lemon walls and filled it with the things that babies need. Most of these had come from friends and neighbours in the village. Betty had been overwhelmed with offers of cots and prams and inundated with assorted knitted baby clothes. Some of which she secretly thought a tad garish but was too kind hearted to refuse.

Betty Bin's daughter was christened in St Urith's church with her grandmother Ruby who was to be one of the godmothers at her side, wearing an expression on her face that dared anybody to question who the father was. Aunty Margaret was there with her son Harold the cross-dressing librarian, who was Betty's cousin.

The family were used to Harold and his little ways and they loved his individual style and joie-de-vivre. Never normally worried or embarrassed there was however a little frisson of concern as to what he might be wearing on this occasion, as it was in church.

Betty still had nightmares about a previous badminton tournament which took place in the parish hall. Harold had turned up in a white tennis skirt, a pink push-up bra visible through his white chiffon blouse, a pair of pink trimmed ankle socks, white plimsolls and a pink bow in his hair.

Betty and the rest of the badminton club were familiar and comfortable with his usual attire but the see-through chiffon blouse was new and nobody, least of all Betty was prepared for the occasional glimpses of neon pink thong as he dashed around the court.

Betty and Ruby however were delighted this time with Harold's outfit for the christening, especially as he was to be the Godfather. He had chosen vintage, a rather fetching peach satin cocktail dress with coordinating shrug and a pair of matching kitten-heeled satin shoes. The whole ensemble topped off with a fascinating fascinator of peach feathers and beading.

The second godmother was Audrey Boy, PCSO Boy's mother. She had been to school with Betty and although she had been a couple of years ahead, they had been best friends. She was a great support to Betty as she had been in the same situation, the result of which was Billy. However it was thought in the village that Audrey was a bit of a one. The gossips say she still has a relationship with Billy's father or how else would she manage to wear such nice clothes and have a new car every year. The truth she kept to herself apart from her friend Betty. Her secret was she made the most exquisite hand stitched lingerie for the rich and famous.

There had been a good turnout in the church, the

promise of food and drink in the nearby social club afterwards probably helped. Most people even managed to suppress their chuckles when the vicar named the baby.

"I baptise you Dusty Urith Bins." Dusty managed not to cry or be sick over the christening gown Celia had knitted for her and everybody piled into the club for a bit of a knees up afterwards. Betty had eventually taken over the bakery from Ruby and changed the sign over the door from 'Bins Bakery' to Betty Bins Buns & Batch.

Dusty was following in her mother's and grandmother's footsteps. A modern young woman, after leaving catering college she trained as a patissiere and was desperate to expand the range of cakes in the bakery from the one bun. Although she was determined to achieve it one day, Dusty knew it would take something monumentous to move her stubborn mother.

27

BILLY GIVES CHASE

Although Billy hadn't spotted Nico leaving the house, he had noticed the strange car parked up the road and had called it in. He discovered that it was a hire car rented from Bristol Airport. Billy opened his window and in the quiet of the village night, heard a car start up and saw the lights of the suspicious car come on. As it passed him he quickly tipped his cup of tea out of the window and passed his bun to Dusty, then in his wing mirror he saw the car stop and somebody come out of the field and climb into it.

"Dusty, put your seatbelt on quickly." Billy had made a split-second decision as to whether to stay on watch outside the victim's houses as the inspector had instructed or follow the car. "Hold tight." Billy started his mum's Corsa, accelerated up the road and executing a handbrake turn at the monument followed the car. Keeping a fair distance away because once out of the village he knew there were no streetlights and he would be more noticeable.

Billy asked Betty to ring the Inspector on his mobile

phone, telling him that a suspect had left the village with a man in a hired car and PCSO Boy was in pursuit.

"There's no answer, I'll send him a text. Billy this is so exciting, it's like being in an episode of 'Heartbeat'."

"But that's set in the 60s."

"Yeah I know but I love the music and the clothes they wear and it's set in the countryside similar to ours. Can I put some music on to make it more authentic?"

"Dusty this isn't a tv soap. It's serious, three people have been murdered!"

"Three! I thought it was just the Colonel and the man in the graveyard!" She replied. "who's the third one?"

"It's not meant to be public knowledge yet but I expect by this time everyone in the village knows. It's Pinky Pope."

"Oh no, poor Pinky. But why? Sometimes he was a bit grumpy but he was always kind to us when we were kids."

Feeling rather important Billy answered "We're not sure yet but we think he may have seen something of the Colonel's murderer."

"Oh Billy, I'm scared, it's not exciting anymore." Dusty grabbed his arm and leaned her head on it.

"Don't worry Dusty, I'll protect you, I won't let anyone hurt you. We're not going to get close to them anyway, we're going to keep our distance."

Dusty who already had a severe crush on Billy, fell head-over-heels in love at the words 'I'll protect you' and didn't really hear the last bit. She relaxed back into the seat as gooey as a sucked marshmallow, her head resting on one side gazing at his adorable profile, whilst Billy attempted to concentrate on following the twin red lights ahead of him in the dark.

28

MURDEROUS INTENT

The murderer hiding in the Cottle's garden had also seen Dottie leaving. In fact Dottie had passed by within a short distance of the hiding place but in her hurry to get away hadn't noticed anybody concealed in the bushes. The murderer heard a car pull away followed by a second car starting up, a screeching in the distance then the engine sounds fading as they left the village. She was incensed because she had been about to go in and tackle Dottie when Nico arrived. Knowing that she wouldn't be able to deal with them both on her own, she had waited in her hiding place, then unexpectedly Nico left followed by Dottie. The killer had an idea and made for the person who could be used as a means to the end.

29

A G & T AT LAST

Celia went straight to her bedroom when she arrived home, changed into her pyjamas and put her slippers on before going to find Ronald. He was waiting in the kitchen holding out a drink in a tall glass with a piece of lime and some ice cubes floating at the top.

"Ronald you are a lifesaver, that's just what I need, thank you."

"Your dinners in the oven." Said Ronald. "It might be a bit dried up by now but you must eat. I've laid up a place on the table you go and sit down and I'll bring it into you."

"You're a hero, thanks Ronald." Celia took her gin and tonic into the living room and sat down at the dining table. She felt bone-weary, it had been an exhausting day and she was glad that for her it was over and she was safe in her own home. Sipping her drink a myriad of thoughts were buzzing in her head. The only way she thought she could make sense of any of it was to look at her list and write a few things down.

She went to fetch her notebook and pen but as she crossed the hall to go to her bag she noticed a piece of white paper lying on the doormat. She picked it up but didn't look at it as she thought that it was probably a notice of an event in the social club as usual.

Sitting back at the table she opened the list she had made earlier in the day and in a fresh notebook started to doodle and write down some notes, not in any order but just as she thought of them.

The first doodle was a lawnmower. The Colonel's death - Very strange circumstances. Why so many visits to the recycling centre? Why was he suddenly interested in eco building? Dottie said he seemed jollier, was he seeing someone? Someone at the dump?

Suspects - Dorothy/wife, Pinky + Unknown person

The dead man in the churchyard - Was he Willy's 'furriner'? Who is he and where does he come from? He certainly wasn't a local but he wasn't necessarily a foreigner as Willy thought not in today's multiracial England. Celia drew a headstone next to him.

The next doodle was a Pope's mitre next to it she wrote.

Pinky - What did he see? - What did he know that may have got him killed?

Postcard - It must have been for Dottie but who was the postcard from and what was its significance? No doodle here just GREECE in capital letters.

There must be some connection between these victims but blowed if she could see it. After looking at it for a while she realised she was too tired and no further forward. She decided that she would sleep on it and then after a good night's rest look at it again in the morning.

Pushing the notepad away from her she knocked the piece of paper that had been posted through her door off the table. She bent down to pick it up and opened it reading.

IF YOU VALUE THE LIFE OF THAT FOUR LEGGED MUTT

KEEP YOUR BIG NOSE OUT OF THE COTTLES COTTAGE

Always slightly self-conscious and sensitive about her nose the insult was as nothing to the anger and panic she felt at the murderous intent to Hirsute Roley. Thrusting her chair back she rose and searched the living room for her little furry baby. Usually he was in his favourite spot sitting on his little cushion on the window sill, watching the world go by!

She raced to the kitchen unfortunately colliding with Ronald who was just bringing her dinner through. The plate went flying through the air and landed upside down of course and in several pieces, food everywhere, luckily they didn't have carpets. Ronald wearing a fair amount of gravy and bits of dinner down his white T-shirt was taken aback and let out a few interesting words but Celia didn't give him any time for questions.

"Where's Hirsute Roley, quick, oh get out of the way." Not giving Ronald a chance to answer, she pushed him aside and shot out of the back door.

Ronald rushed after her, Celia shouting at him that someone had stolen their beloved dog. Together they searched but there was no sign of the little dog in the house, garden or out in the road, which they searched from top to bottom.

They walked back home. Celia was crying as she gave Ronald the note. He read it, angry and frightened for

Hirsute Roley he said. "You see this is what happens when you start interfering in murders."

"What a bloody unfair thing to say! Don't you dare say this is my fault! Don't you think I feel bad enough as it is? And what was I supposed to do ignore Dottie when she rang this morning?" Celia was distraught.

"I'm sorry you're right, come here." Ronald opened his arms and Celia stepped into them and sobbed on his shoulder. After a few minutes she wiped her eyes, blew her nose and pulling herself together said. " I know you won't like this Ronald but I *have* to find out who the killer is. Even more now that bastard has got little Hirsute Roley! I couldn't bear it if he was hurt" 'or even worse' hung in the air but wasn't said out loud.

"I understand how you feel, I feel as bad as you do Celia but we must let the police handle this. We must contact them straight away. Do you realise that this person knows where you live and was bold enough to come to our home to kidnap Hirsute Roley. You're in danger and I won't let you risk your life, even for our baby! Look at it out there, it's getting dark and it certainly isn't a good idea to go wandering about the village with a murderer on the loose."

"Yes of course. I suppose you're right but it will be very hard not to do anything. I'll go and ring the inspector." Celia went to fetch the phone.

"Then make yourself a sandwich. "Said Ronald. "You need to eat and it will give you something to do. I'll pour you another gin. It is going to be hard you're right, but we must leave it to the experts. We'll watch a bit of telly, take our mind off things." Ronald poured himself another glass of wine and went through to the living room. He switched on the telly, settled down on the sofa, a worried frown on his face and let the tears that he had been holding back fall.

At the same time Celia stood looking out of the kitchen window into the darkening garden, tears slowly dripped down her cheeks as she thought of her dear little dog. He looked a bit like a teddy bear, he had such a sweet little face, waggy tail and cheerful personality, such a dear little dog. It didn't matter how long they'd left him, when they returned home he was always excited to see them. Always happy when he was around them both, she knew he must be scared and confused wherever he was being kept. She could only hope that whoever had him wouldn't harm a hair on his dear little head.

She made herself a cup of tea but not the sandwich, there was no way she could eat anything, she was too upset. Unbearable though it was she knew Ronald was right and that there was no point in rushing around trying to find Hirsute Roley, there were too many places he could be hidden.

She spotted his favourite stuffed toy under the bar stool and the tears started again. It was no good, she would wait a while, hope that Ronald would doze off as usual and then she would make her way to Dottie's. She had a feeling that Hirsute Roley and the murderer wouldn't be far away from the Cottles house. Damn! she suddenly remembered that Dottie was meant to be coming to stay the night. Drying her eyes and blowing her nose again, she fetched bedding from the blanket chest and made up the bed in the spare room. Hopefully Ronald would be asleep by the time she had finished.

She left the bedroom curtains open whilst she was making the bed, so that she would see if the outside light came on, she wanted to catch Dottie before she rang the front door bell and woke Ronald up.

Ronald was asleep. Dottie had rung up to say that she really appreciated Celia's offer but had decided to stay at home after all. She hadn't been able to get hold of the inspector. When she rang his mobile phone it went straight to answerphone, so she had left a message. It was time.

Now dark outside except for the streetlights, Celia stepped out of the house and paused before closing the door. She looked down at the spot that little Hirsute Roley would normally be, holding his paw up, asking to go with her in his own doggy way with a woof, woof.

Chapter Thirty Five - Celia Ventures Forth

Closing the door quietly behind her, the outside light came on as she walked down the path and out of the gate. Celia was aware that she was probably being watched. She stood for a moment, nervous and not a hundred percent sure she was doing the right thing. Going out in the night on her own was dangerous but she also knew she couldn't go to bed as if nothing had happened. Not really having a plan as such but thinking that Dottie's house was where she needed to be, she set off.

Steeling herself to be brave she turned in the direction of the unlit alley that connected Celia's road with the square. It would have been safer to walk the other way, down the road and through the village, lit by the streetlights but this way she was less likely to be seen.

As Celia reached the darkened alley she switched on her trusty torch and slowly scanned from side to side across the narrow path. She was scared, the killer knew

The Curious Curiosity 171

who she was, where she lived and had been bold enough to enter her garden and kidnap Hirsute Roley. The killer could be watching her now! All her senses were on high alert and she was not stupid enough *not* to be cautious with a killer on the loose. Especially as the killer had managed to murder two strong fit men not including Pinky who probably hadn't been aware of the killer creeping up behind him.

God she was scared, walking forward slowly, she began to feel very uneasy. Not at her best in the dark, Celia found even the torch wasn't helping. It seemed to create even darker pools of menacing dark that a killer could hide in.

She had almost reached the junction at the top of the alley and now felt trapped between the two walls on either side and another up ahead. With darkness up front and darkness behind she stopped frozen for a moment, then swirled around with her torch, waving it wildly to and fro. Finding nothing behind her she still couldn't shake off the feeling that someone was out there with her. She felt she had no choice but to carry on and was glad she always went for a cotton gusset.

Celia's sixth sense was right. The murderer, watching, could see Celia was nervous by her slow progress and the wildly swinging torch. Smiling from a concealed spot behind the tree near to the entrance to the alley, this was just what the murderer wanted. It had been the right plan to steal her dog.

Celia couldn't hear a thing as she reached the part of the alley where it met the cross section, just the sound of a tractor silaging through the night and the inevitable dogs barking. To the right the path led down past the backs of the bungalows to the main road below but it was unlit and pitch black. As she stepped forward she shone her torch down it, just in case someone was waiting to hit her over the head and startled a small black cat who looked up without releasing the half dead thing under it's paw. Turning back to her left she walked towards the light from a small street lamp that stood on guard at the end of the alleyway.

Before this night she had always felt comfortable walking around the village at night. It made her angry that the killer had taken that away from her. As she reached the light she turned her torch off and walked quietly across the square, glancing at the church as she passed. Keeping close to the hedges she made her way around the village towards the Cottle's cottage, where she knew Billy would be on watch.

The killer must still be in the village for a reason, Celia thought. They hadn't found what it was they were searching for and they were getting more desperate, hence the murder of poor Pinky. More and more she was convinced the answer lay at the Cottles cottage. If one ignored the body in the churchyard for the moment, everything else centred around the Cottle's house. The Colonel's and Pinky's death. The fact Dottie was sure the house had been searched and she was convinced Dottie was keeping something back. Then there was the mystery of the postcard.

All this was swirling around Celia's mind as she walked through the village. Turning the corner into the Cottle's road, the first thing she noticed and which stopped her in her tracks, was that PCSO Boy was *not* on watch outside of the Cottle's. Well his mother's car wasn't there and she was sure she remembered the Inspector telling her Billy would borrow it.

Celia's first thought was to worry about Dottie alone in the house, on her own without any protection. Increasing her pace she made her way to the Cottles.

Chapter Thirty Six - Celia Confronted

The curtains were closed in the living room and there was no light on. She cautiously made her way around the side of the house towards the kitchen door. The Kitchen curtains were closed but there was a light on, unfortunately there were no gaps or chinks to peep through.

Celia knocked gently on the door not wanting to frighten Dottie. After waiting a couple of minutes she knocked again a little harder when suddenly she was attacked from behind. An arm was pressing around her throat and something hard was digging into her back. She was only wearing a thin grey cardigan over the top of her summer pyjamas because the hot day had turned into a mild night. It wasn't long before the tip of the knife penetrated that and her top cutting into her flesh.

Shocked and cross with herself for dropping her guard Celia shouted "Let go of me at once!"

"Keep quiet and you won't get hurt." A soft feminine voice said into her ear.

"You're already hurting me! That knife is cutting into me!"

The killer pulled the knife away. "Now shut up. Under that pot is the door key, reach down slowly, no sudden moves, I won't hesitate to use this."

Celia slowly moved down towards the pot still with the arm tight around her throat and aware of the knife hovering at her side.

"Now unlock the door."

Celia fumbled with the key. "You won't get away with this, there's a policeman on watch out there and he's probably called for reinforcements! Her hands were shaking, she was terrified but at least the knife was no longer cutting into her.

"Nice try but you're little policeman is all loved up with some girl, they've gone off in the car for a little session somewhere." The woman said as she pushed Celia up the step, through the door and into the brightly lit kitchen.

"Where's Dottie? What have you done with her?

"Calm down grandma, I haven't done anything with her, ... yet."

The woman dragged Celia over to a kitchen chair, hoiking it out with her foot and pushing her down onto it. "Now sit down and shut up."

There was a loud crack and pain shot through Celia's shoulders as her arms were dragged behind her.

"Ow what was that?" the woman asked in a surprisingly concerned voice.

"My shoulder." Groaned Celia.

"Oh, I'm really sorry. Would you rather I tied your hands in front instead?"

Surprised at the woman's kindness considering she was very likely the murderer of three people, Celia answered "yes please." then thought why am I saying please, for goodness sake?

The woman tied Celia's hands together efficiently with a black industrial plastic tie, tight enough that there was no wriggle-room. Then she pulled out a blue and white patterned headscarf, taking an end in each hand she whirled it around and around until it was a thick material rope.

Celia had read enough murder stories to realise that this was a gag and protested. "Please don't put anything in my mouth, I suffer from catarrh and blocked sinuses and I won't be able to breathe properly." She was beginning to realise that she probably would not be getting out of Dottie's house alive. Where was Dottie? The killer hadn't checked if there had been anybody in the house so she must know that there wasn't.

The woman hesitated " I won't gag you if you promise not to shout, scream or anything else, because if you do I will not hesitate to stop you. For good!"

"I promise." This is bizarre thought Celia, she's obviously a ruthless killer without a conscience and wouldn't hesitate to use the knife on me but she is also showing a little kindness. Perhaps there's a chance I might survive. Just then Andrea Bocelli sang out 'Funiculi Funicula' from her bag, making them both jump.

"What the hell is that?" The killer shouted agitated and waving the knife about.

Celia trying to contain her fear and keep the killer calm said. "It's just my phone."

"Why on earth would you have a ringtone like that?" The woman asked.

Andrea kept singing until eventually he stopped.

"I'd forgotten I'd changed it when I left here earlier. It's probably my husband. I left without telling him where I was going. If I don't ring him back he'll assume I've come around here and he'll get in his car and be around here in a few seconds to make sure I'm alright."

"Kolos! OK this is what we're going to do, you are going to ring him back and tell him you are here OK, talking to your friend."

The woman grabbed Celia's bag and tipped it out onto the table, a ball of wool fell out and rolled off the edge, followed by the knitting needle it was attached to. A notebook, pens, tissues, a diary, the second needle and finally a mobile phone lying on the top. Reaching out the woman picked up the phone, pressed call-back and held it against Celia's ear, at the same time putting the point of the knife against her throat. "Tell your husband you are safe, reassure him, One wrong word and..." She pressed the knife into Celia's neck drawing a small bead of blood.

Celia felt sick, her throat so tight she was not sure if she could even speak to Ronald. With tears in her eyes she took a deep breath tried to relax her shoulders and forced herself to stay calm.

"Hello? Hello?" Shouted Ronald.

"Ronald It's me, Celia."

"Where are you? Why did you go out without telling me? I was worried about you. Are you OK?"

"Yes I'm fine."

"What? Say again, you sound a bit odd." Ronald queried.

Celia raised her voice "I said, I'm fine." She felt the knife dig into her neck "He's a bit deaf, he can't hear me very well, that's all." The pressure eased off her neck.

"Who are you talking to? Are you at Dotties? is she there?"

"Yes I am but Dotties not. Don't worry, I'll be home soon."

"Dotties not there! But how did you get in and who's with you? Something's wrong isn't it? Celia I'm going to call the Inspector, don't move, I'm coming," The line went dead.

"Ronald don't come around I'm OK!" Celia shouted but Ronald had gone. The last thing Celia wanted was Ronald to put himself in danger as well. She carried on talking. "Yes, yes, I'm fine, OK I'll see you later." Thank God he would call the inspector.

She knew she was in a desperate situation but she certainly didn't intend to die at the hands of this strange woman. She thought that the woman looked a little familiar but she couldn't place her. Buying time is what she needed to do according to most of the crime dramas on TV or in books but as it happened she didn't need to do that because unbeknown to Celia, the killer needed her alive.

"What is it you want from me?" Celia asked as she was dragged up by her tied hands.

"I want what was stolen from my family."

"Well I haven't got whatever it is that's been stolen from your family you stupid woman, I've never met you before in my life!"

"You're the stupid one, poking your nose into things that are no business of yours."

"It's all Greek to me." Celia said hoping to touch a nerve.

"So now you are taking the piss out of me because I am Greek! Just remember lady that I have the power and I am in control here." The woman shouted back.

"Thank you for remembering I'm a lady." Celia said primly.

"Enough of this rubbish talk. Shut up!" The woman was clearly losing her temper.

Celia wasn't sure if this was a good thing or a bad one. "Hmph quite obviously you are not a lady." Celia pushed again, deciding that getting the woman angry was the right thing. If she could goad her enough she might make a mistake. Then something clicked. "Rubbish! That's where I remember you from. You work at the recycling centre."

The woman pushed Celia up against the dresser and held the knife to her throat again. "I warn you, I don't want to gag you but I will if you don't stop talking. We haven't got much time."

"*We* haven't got much time, don't include me in your plans." Celia gasped out, wondering if she had gone too far.

"God, you are the most infuriating woman I have ever met!" The woman let Celia go and angrily strode away to the opposite end of the kitchen.

"Infuriating *lady*, if you don't mind and what have you done with Dottie and Hirsute Roley?" Celia asked in her most dignified manner.

"Who the hell is Hirsute Roley?" The woman asked exasperatedly.

"My dog! You kidnapped him didn't you."

"You are completely mad aren't you? If you do as I say you'll get your skylos back. Now sit down!" The woman pushed her back onto the kitchen chair.

Chapter Thirty Seven - Keep Calm & Carry On

Celia sat on the kitchen chair with her back to the door, the woman was standing on the other side of the table. Celia endeavouring to stay calm and keep alive asked "So tell me, do you think that whatever has been stolen from your family is either in this house or Pinky's house?"

"What the hell is this Pinky?" Asked the woman.

Before Celia could answer they both heard a noise, it came from outside the back door. Everything happened in a moment. Celia started shouting out a warning thinking it was Ronald. "Ronald don't come in!" but was stopped from saying anything further by the woman who ran across and put the knife to her throat just as the door opened and Dottie and Nico burst through.

"Celia!" Dottie called out in dismay "Oh God are you alright? What's happening? Who are you and what are you doing in my house?"

"You, shut up, Nico, sit down or she get's hurt."

Dottie looked at Nico, terror in her eyes. Nico was weighing up the chances of overpowering the woman without Celia being harmed but decided the risk was too much. He pulled out a chair and sat down. Then it hit him, the woman had called him Nico, how did she know his name he didn't think he recognised her?

"You." The woman said to Dottie, "Take this and tie his hands behind his back." She threw another plastic tie across the table.

Dottie couldn't make her legs work, she was frozen to the spot.

"Now! shouted the woman.

Dottie flinched.

"It's OK Dottie, do as she says, it's going to be OK." Reassured Nico.

Making a huge effort to control her fear Dottie reached over the table and picked up the plastic tie. Nico started to get up out of his chair but the woman dug the knife into Celia's neck.

"I'm warning you, now sit down!"

Nico dropped back into his seat and put his hands behind his back so that Dottie could loop the tie around. There was something about the woman that was familiar, more than her accent, which he'd recognised straight away but he just couldn't place her.

"Stand up and let me see her tie it properly." The woman ordered Nico.

Nico stood up and turned around so that the woman could see Dottie pull the tie tight.

"Now sit down both of you!"

They both sat. Dottie was relieved that it didn't look as if she would have her hands tied behind her back but was very worried as to what would happen next.

Celia was wondering where Ronald had got to. She thought he might be here by now but then in a way she was relieved he wasn't because she knew that he wouldn't hesitate to try and rescue her, even if it was dangerous. She hoped he'd called the Inspector first though, he wasn't stupid enough to think that he could deal with the situation on his own.

In fact Ronald had arrived but had been prevented from entering the Cottle's by the Inspector and PCSO Boy who were there before him.

Chapter Thirty Eight - Calling in the Cavalry

" Now don't you worry Mr Ladygarden. Can I call you Ronald? (Ronald nodded) I know the situation looks bad." The Inspector paused. " In fact it is bad and it could get worse. I can't get hold of any reinforcements and we can't take a chance and wait for the armed response unit. Goodness knows how long it will take them to get here from Exeter.

The killer has already taken at least three lives that we know of and probably won't mind taking an....."

Ronald interrupted "Yes Ok Inspector I get the picture. Thanks for the reassurance!"

"That's OK Ronald. Now Boy let's try ringing PCSO Clapp, I know she's off duty but see if she is near enough to join us, that will make three of us."

"Yes sir, straight away sir." PCSO Boy moved away from the Inspector to make his call. Away from the growing crowd of villagers who had come along to see what was going on.

"Better than telly this." Said one

"What's going on then?" Asked another.

"I ave it on good authority that Pinky Pope went mad with lust for that thur Trixie Bell."

"Cor er's a roight booty enmp't she?" Leered another

"Depends on who's yer fancy I reckon. But anyway parently he went ont rampage and killed ten people and now ee's got ol Celia in there and he's goin to ave ee's way with er."

"Get on." Acknowledge another.

"Honestly you lot take the biscuit!" It was Veronica who burst out of the hedge into the middle of the gossiping group with a bramble tangled in her blonde hair and waving a bunch of stinging nettles in her hand.

"Who was this good authority then? Asked Veronica thrusting the nettles around into the faces the three men who had been enjoying the drama.

"Well it was ole Fred at the 'Unkempt Muff' responded the first informant"

"And I suppose you believe old Fred when he tells you he doesn't water down his beer and cleans his pumps out every week?" Veronica said.

There was a bit of mumbling and cursing until Veronica pulled out her hip flask and offered it around.

They might be enjoying the fermented fruits of Veronica's foraging now but in the morning they might wonder what the bloody hell hit them.

Before PCSO Boy could ring for PCSO Clapp he had to get a decent signal. There were so many places that you couldn't get a signal in St Urith, it was a going to be a matter of luck. High-speed broadband was a little slow in coming.

30

AUNTIE PAT TO THE RESCUE.

PCSO Claire Clapp was enjoying her evening in the 'Cavalier's Hose' named for the Civil War history in the town. It was one of her favourite haunts and after eating a chicken curry and a few drinks she was now playing pool with her best friend Daisy. She was winning when Billy rang her on her mobile. Taking out her phone she saw it was Billy rejected the call and put it back in her pocket. She was just taking her next shot when her phone went off again. Seeing it was Billy again she answered it and stuck it between her ear and shoulder as she went to take the next shot.

"Billyboy! what do you want, you're putting me off my shot."

"Claire it's Billy."

"Yes Billy I know. I may not be a fully-fledged policewoman but I can read your name on my mobile. Getting bored are you? Want to join me and Daisy in the Cavalier's Hose? You know she fancies you."

Billy could hear Daisy calling out 'hello Billy' in the background.

"Does she? oh forget about that Claire this is urgent, a police matter."

"But I'm not on duty!" Claire protested.

"I know that but this is serious." Said Billy.

"Really Billy, how exciting, what's up?" Claire put down her cue and leaned against the pool table.

"Claire we have a hostage situation. The perp is holding a woman in a cottage in St Urith" Billy said importantly.

"The perp?" Claire couldn't help it, she giggled "Oh Billy you make me laugh. You've been watching too much CSI on telly."

"Yea, OK, whatever. But I am being deadly serious Claire. The perp…person really is holed up in a house with a hostage. We really do need your help there's only me and Inspector Burke here."

"Burke by name burk by nature."

"This is so not funny. Have you been drinking Claire? where are you?"

"You haven't been listening, I'm in the pub with Daisy and yes I've had a few." She paused. "Are you *really* serious Billy?"

"Yes I am Claire. We really need your help in St Urith but you can't drive if you've been drinking. Is there anyone who can give you a lift? And don't ask anyone in the pub."

"I'll go and ask aunty Pat, she's the nearest, I'll be there as soon as."

"Your aunty Pat! but she's eighty two! and probably in bed by now!"

"Yes but she's the nearest and she's game for anything!" Claire cut off the call and said to Daisy. "I've got to go, urgent police business." She gathered up her jacket and bag and started towards the door of the pub.

"But what about me?" Whined Daisy.

"C'mon, you can come too and then you can stay in the car and look after aunty Pat."

"Aunty Pat? Why am I looking after aunty Pat? Asked Daisy.

It wasn't long before all three were heading for the village in aunty Pat's red Peugeot, which was so old it was like riding in an old armchair on rockers. Aunty Pat was driving and even though it was summer and a warm night she was wearing a fleecy leopard onesie with the bottom of the legs cut off because she said it made her ankles hot. On her feet she sported white jelly sandals with her green painted toenails peeking out. Her hair was dyed a rather scary shade of fiery orange and was sporting three pink rollers, one in her fringe and one each side of her face.

"Thank you for this aunty Pat, you're a star and I really appreciate it. I'm sorry you didn't have time to get dressed but according to Billy this is a hostage situation!" Explained Claire

"Oh don't you worry about that, this is the most excitement since Mr Mc Loosely was a guest at our WI."

"Goodness really?What on earth was his talk about?" Asked Claire.

" He gave us a talk on surviving in the wild. It was all a bit boring until he was telling us how to forage for food that's safe to eat, when Marjorie Phipps who quite frankly Claire could survive on her own excess body fat for at least three months..."

"That's a bit harsh Aunty."

"But true Claire. Anyway on the pretext of going to the toilet she nose-dived into the tuna vol-au-vents and cut-rounds. Irene Ingles, '*madam*' chairperson was furious and started to get up to go and stop her. The other ladies who hadn't really been listening or paying attention to poor Mr Mc Loosley started to rise up out of their seats as well, thinking the talk was over. They didn't want to miss out on the refreshments and knowing that Marjorie had got there first they knew there wouldn't be much left by the time they got there. Mr Mc Loosely realised he was losing his audience, so picking up two sticks he loudly banged them together shouting 'LET'S MAKE FIRE!'

The trouble was Wendy Wood who was in the front row had become bored and drifted off to sleep. Completely relaxed she'd slipped down a bit in her seat, her knees had strayed East and West and poor Mr Mc Loosely had a view of her rather racy red satin clad Khyber Pass."

Aunty Pat's eyes squeezed closed occasionally as she roared with laughter in between telling the story. To the consternation of Daisy who hung on to the arm rest and just managed to stop herself from telling Claire's aunt to keep her eyes on the road, knowing it would be a waste of her breath.

"Oh my God, that's hysterical!" Laughed Claire.

"It get's better dear. Unfortunately Wendy is slightly hard of hearing and she only heard the word 'Fire' shouted by Mr Mc Loosely, who by the way happened to be wearing pale linen trousers.

"Uh?" Queried Claire

"The shout woke Wendy up. She jumped , launched her full bottle of elderflower water, (she's been on a bit of a health kick) at Mr Mc Loosely whose trousers went completely transparent. The stampede for the buffet had stopped in it's tracks when he shouted fire and everyone had turned back to see what was what. That's when we discovered Mr Mc Loosely dresses commando style. It was the most exciting talk we've ever had at the WI . Throw your blue light on top of the roof love and I'll put me foot down."

Claire who along with Daisy was laughing so hard she was crying, wasn't sure if she had heard her aunty right. "I haven't got a blue light aunty."

"Starsky and Hutch always had a blue light! The Sweeney always had a blue light. You're the police, you must have a blue light!"

Thinking it was best not to argue Claire agreed. "Well yes of course I *have* got a blue light aunty but this is an undercover operation."

"Well why didn't you say so love, right, hang on to your undies girls. I'll keep a low profile just like the MFI!" Aunty Pat adjusted her driving seat so that she was virtually lying almost horizontally and put her jelly-shoed foot hard down on the accelerator.

Pulled back by the G-force Claire protested. "Slow down aunty! You can't see where you're going lying down like that!"

"Of course I can" aunty Pat said indignantly "I can see through the gap in the steering wheel!"

31

THE GATHERING OF THE MASSES

By now there were even more villagers gathering under the street lights, agog as to what was going on. All sorts of rumours were flowing around, fuelled by Willy and his talk of furriners and strange goings on. Some were saying Celia had been arrested, others that Dottie had killed the Colonel and was holding Celia hostage until she got a getaway helicopter. That caused consternation as who would write the village panto if Celia was murdered. Some of the teenagers thought it would be cool if a helicopter landed.

Then Trixie Bell arrived with the news that Pinky Pope was not the murderer. In fact he was the one who had been brutally murdered in his own home.

This caused Mrs Finch, Birdie to her friends, to collapse shrieking into the one arm of Willy, who failed to hold on to the poor woman even though she had a tiny frame. Mrs Finch's tiny hand inadvertently slipped through the baler twine bow that was holding up Willy's trousers, causing a catastrophic effect.

Luckily Max Cheetham moving swiftly but gracefully,

managed to catch birdie against his virile frame. Max had only recently moved into the village and was considered by the ladies to be quite the silverfox. Although there had been plenty of speculation and despite various visits to his door by the ladies of the village bringing welcoming casseroles, as yet, nobody had been able to find out anything about his background, or why he had chosen to live in St Urith.

There was a collective indrawing of breath at the sight of Max sweeping Birdie off her feet from the women present and Harold the cross-dressing librarian and his pen-pal Vincent who was paying a surprise visit from Brazil. Vincent had obviously dashed out in a hurry as he appeared to be wearing only the one item of clothing, a brightly coloured Harlequin patterned silk dressing gown. His dark, smooth as a baby's bottom chest and legs were exposed to the evening air and the whole contained only by a flimsy belt tied in a loose knot.

Miss Worsnip pushed her way through the crowd and bustled importantly up to the Inspector, jabbing him in the back with a scrawny digit. As the Inspector turned around in response, the digit jabbed it's way into his chest. "Are we all going to be murdered in our beds now? That's three murders! What are you going to do about it? I pay my taxes you know!"

The Inspector arrested her bony arm in mid air as it fast approached his chest for the second time. "Madam take a hold of yourself, you can't go around attacking policeman!"

"Owo ow, police brutality, let me go, ow, ow, I'll put the law on to you!" Miss Worsnip whined.

Trixie coming to the Inspector's rescue, took Miss Worsnip's arm gently from the Inspector and said soothingly. "He is the law Miss Worsnip and you cannot go around jabbing people, especially not the police, you'll get yourself arrested."

Several voices obviously agreed with Miss Worsnip as there were cries of "Yea but she's right though isn't she? Yea what you be doin just anging rownd. And "Ee be maized as a brush"

The Inspector tried to hush the crowd but the mutterings just got louder. "As if things weren't bad enough this is turning into an effing farce!" He complained.

Billy thought he'd better do something before things got out of hand. Dusty had been helping him to keep the crowd back , he took her to one side and whispered into her ear. She slipped away to find her mother and in turn whispered in her ear. After a few minutes there was an ear-piercing whistle that shut everyone up apart from one wag who asked. "Is that Celia's whistle, it must be panto time!" followed by another would-be comedian who shouted "Oh no it isn't!"

"This isn't the time for jokes, or for accusations either. This is serious, " Betty Bins said looking directly at Miss Worsnip. "Let's all settle down and listen to what the Inspector has to say. Remember there have already been several deaths and we don't want any more. Especially not our dear friend Celia." Her voice choked on the last words and Dusty put her arm around her mother, hugging her tightly.

The Inspector jumped into the pool of silence that followed Betty's words before anyone else decided they wanted a say. " Thank you Mrs Bins, I appreciate your help. Now listen up everybody Mrs Bins is right. I understand you're all frightened and worried and you have every right to be. The situation is very serious. Against regulations and normal procedures I am going to tell you what's going on and I ask for all of you to co-operate as lives are at stake."

There was a short burst of chatter, mutterings and gasps at this information and then everyone settled down to listen to what the Inspector had to say.

"First of all will you all turn off your mobile phones, we need everyone to be focussed and not busy texting or taking photos." The Inspector waited, nothing happened for a few minutes and then Betty Bins pulled out her phone and made a great show of turning it off. Everyone else soon followed. Nobody stopped Miss Worsnip when she hurried off muttering about turning off her home phone.

The Inspector resumed "Mrs Ladygarden, Celia, is being held in the Cottle's house under duress."

"Good God! What's he saying? Celia's lost her dress." Ronald sunk his head in his hands, at the thought, knowing that Celia probably didn't have a bra on. He'd forgotten she was wearing pyjamas when she left home but then, most days he wouldn't have been able to tell anyone what she was wearing anyway.

Billy reassured him speaking loudly. "It's OK Ronald, he says she's being held under duress. She is being held hostage."

"Well why didn't he say so then? but that doesn't make me feel any better Billy."

"Harumph!" The Inspector cleared his throat and waited for silence once again. "As you can see there is only myself, PCSO Boy and hopefully one other officer who will be joining us shortly. We have to assume that reinforcements may not arrive in time, working together, we can make sure nobody else dies."

"Inspector!" Said Ronald. "I'm not liking your choice of words. 'May not arrive in time' and 'hopefully no one dies'. This is my wife you are talking about. Why aren't reinforcements here? There should be armed police swarming all over the place and a helicopter overhead. What do you think you can do with a couple of young PCSO's and a bunch of villager? No disrespect intended."

"Ronald, I'm sorry. I have requested assistance but we have to act as if they may not arrive in time. I have years of experience in these situations and although PCSO Boy and PCSO Clapp are young, they are also bright, brave and willing to do what it takes to rescue your wife." He turned to the crowd.

"I am asking you all to help and assist us with this dreadful situation. Celia is one of your own and I am positive that if you all do as I ask we will be able to rescue her and capture the person who has committed these murders."

There was a smattering of applause and murmurings of excited agreement.

"We must keep the noise down, we all need to keep quiet. We don't want to alarm the suspect who we believe is in the Cottles Cottage. Also if you stay quiet you will be able to hear my instructions. Will the able-bodied amongst you who feel they could assist us go and stand next to PCSO Boy." Several men and women moved to stand next to Billy.

The Inspector addressed the remaining group. "Don't worry, the rest of you will be just as useful. I want you to make your silent presence known to the occupants by standing quietly in a group on the path opposite the house and watch. The killer will see you there and know there will be no escape and Celia will know that we are here to help.

Choose one of you to be a runner, er I mean walker to let me know if you see anything happening. Whatever you do, don't shout, don't do anything heroic like trying to rescue Celia. You will only put her in even more danger."

He walked back to PCSO Boy's group which included one-armed Willie who winked at the Inspector at the same time as digging him in the ribs and saying "alroite specter?"

"Yes thank you Mr umm. Right now I want you in pairs, you two go up to the corner and stop any traffic turning into the road." Howard and Vincent headed off down the road with a jaunty wave. "Are they skipping?" The Inspector asked before turning back to the next pair. "And you two go into the field behind and make your way to the back of the cottage but stay down. Lay on your coats if necessary and whatever you do, make sure you cannot be seen."

Robert Bysinger and Ida Cock (Apparently her husband's great grandmother was called Fanny Cock - you couldn't make it up) could barely contain their excitement as they made their way to the field. In their wake was a lot of tittering, sniggering and giggling by the remaining villagers. Everybody in the village knew that Ida's husband worked away and there had been no end of rumours flying around for weeks after the pair had been spotted in several strange positions.

"And you two." The Inspector pointed to Alice and Ella Gurr. "If you could go down to the other end of the road and stop anybody going in or out, that's people and cars, but don't put yourselves in any danger. Have you got anything you could use as a sign or a flag? A handkerchief or something to warn drivers?"

Alice and Ella Gurr looked at each other, grinned and as one reached under their short dresses. They pulled down and stepped out of what to the Inspector looked like pieces of string and waving them gleefully in the air, they set off down the street.

The Inspector started to speak but his voice came out as a squeak, after clearing his voice he carried on. "OK everybody is in place and we are as secure as we can be. The rest of you stay with me, I am going to try and negotiate with the felon but if that doesn't work it may come down to brute strength. I'm hoping it won't come to that and I am fairly sure there are no firearms in the house."

Everybody looked at each other, this was the first they had heard about 'brute strength' and 'firearms'. One of the men stepped backwards away from the group and walked back over to join the watchers. Some of the others were starting to think that might be a good idea but before any more of them could move, there was the sound of an engine.

A speeding car came haring around the corner narrowly missing the girls who had been sent to stop the traffic. It screeched to a halt with a bright orange thong hanging off it's aerial, right in front of the Inspector, whose heart was nearly beating out of his chest. Just as his heart rate was slowing down, the car emitted a storm of sound to the tune of the William Tell Overture. aunty Pat in her excitement at being involved in a police drama and seeing all the people watching had enthusiastically pressed down on her horn several times providing the waiting crowd with extra choruses.

Claire's heart sank as she caught the jaundiced eye of

the Inspector through the passenger window. In her haste she fumbled with the door until it finally opened and she clambered out. "Sorry about that sir, aunty Pat is a little excited."

"*Really* PCSO Clapp I hadn't noticed and I am sure the killer who is holding at *least* one person under duress and whose nerves are probably balanced on a knife edge and whose adrenaline levels are off the scale, hasn't noticed either! What on earth is your aunty doing here anyway?"

The Inspector's voice had risen in scale and volume as he berated poor Claire but in his defence, it was only out of concern for what might be going on inside the cottage.

"Sorry sir, it was the only way I could get here." Explained PCSO Clapp

The Inspector visibly pulled himself together, opened the door of the car and leaned in to speak to aunty Pat. "Madam, thank you for assisting the police, would you help us further by driving your car back up to the end of the road and using it to block the junction? But stay in the car at all times, do not leave your vehicle."

"Oh, my, do I geet a badge?" Enquired aunty Pat

The Inspector was momentarily confused but Claire came to his rescue and spoke over his shoulder. "You'll probably get a bravery award Aunty now off you pop."

Aunty Pat executed the perfect nine point turn and sped off to the end of the road with a flourishing blast of her horn.

The Inspector shook his head as he watched Aunty Pat's rear lights disappear. "PCSO Clapp, I am assuming that was the only transport you could find at such short notice so thank you for coming to our assistance. Don't worry about your aunty she'll be safe enough up there." He sniffed, have you been drinking?"

"Sir! I *was* off duty."

"Yes of course, right, well erm let's get you up to speed. At this present time, we have no idea if there is anyone else in the cottage apart from Mrs Ladygarden and the suspect. I am going to try and negotiate with them"

"Do you think the kidnapper is in there sir?"

"Well of course the kidnapper is in there otherwise why do you think we and half of the village are all standing here? It's not a meeting of the St Urith Astrological Society!" He took a breath as if to calm himself.

"Mrs Ladygarden, spoke to her husband on the telephone from the Cottles and from what he could gather, there was someone else with her. It wasn't Mrs Cottle the occupier of the house, Mrs Ladygarden managed to tell him that much. Mrs Cottle, who is a suspect has disobeyed my instructions to either stay with you or stay in the house until tomorrow when she would come to the station for questioning."

"What were you bringing her in for sir?"

"To formally question her on the murder of her husband, Colonel Cottle."

"What! there's been a murder as well as a kidnapping?" Claire shrieked.

"Well three actually." replied the inspector.

"Three! Oh my God what have I done?" Claire was clearly upset.

"What? You didn't kill anybody. Did you?" Asked the inspector shocked.

"No! Of course not, I just meant I shouldn't have involved Aunty Pat in a mass murder situation. My mum's going to kill me." OOh!" Claire put her hand to her mouth as she realised what she had said.

"Keep your voice down, we don't want to alarm anybody and your Aunty Pat will be fine."

Claire looked around at the gathering crowd and down the road to where aunty Pat was sitting in her car with her hazard lights on, then she turned back the other way to the monument. She could see the outline of a man and a woman standing in the road with their arms outstretched and waving.

"Cooee Claire, isn't this exciting? Called the woman.

Claire tried to make out who it was in the dim light. Then the woman bobbed under a street light and Claire could see she wore a shift dress with a giant sunflower appliqued to the bottom left hand side. A white fluffy knitted bolero adorned her shoulders and on her feet what looked like a pair of sequinned platform sandals that flashed as they caught the light, completing the summer evening look. As the woman lifted her face from under the brim of her white straw hat, the street light revealed Harold the cross-dressing librarian.

"Cooee Harold, love the outfit." Claire called back.

"I'll lend you the pattern love, it's very easy to make as long as you get the neck and the sleeve facings right" Shouted Harold.

Claire was just about to shout back thank you when the Inspector stepped in front of her and said through gritted teeth. "PCSO Clapp you may not have your uniform on but you are still on duty and not at the Great British Sewing Bee! Mrs Ladygarden is probably in danger of her life whilst you are discussing dressmaking at noise levels loud enough to wake Jack the Ripper!" He ended on a shout and there was an immediate.

"Ssshh......." from the villagers.

"Yes sir, sorry sir, I'm all yours sir, what shall I do?"

Surreptitiously she stretched out her arm and made a thumbs up sign to Harold, who thankfully didn't verbally respond.

"I instructed Mrs Cottle not to leave her house except to go to Mrs Ladygardens where she was to stay the night. Unfortunately she took it upon herself to disregard my instructions. But as it happens it was a good job she did, otherwise she would be at risk of losing her life as well as Mrs Ladygarden. Now I want you to get Mrs Cottle's mobile number from Billy and try and see if you can get hold of her. We definitely don't want her to come back home but if she is already on her way, tell her to stop at the end of the road and get in the car with your aunty Pat."

PCSO Clapp did as asked and once she had the number from Billy, pulled her mobile phone out of her Gucci bag bought on holiday in a night market in Teneriffe and entered Dottie's number, wandering around trying to pick up a signal.

Ronald tapped the Inspector on the arm. "I've been very patient Inspector but my wife is in danger in there and apart from shepherding the gawping crowd around you don't seem to be doing anything to get her out of there! I promised her I would come and get her and if you aren't going to do something I am!"

"You're wife wouldn't have been in any danger if she had done as she was told and kept her bloody nose out of things that should have been left to the police!" The Inspector stalked away, anger in every step, he stood looking across the green at the church of Saint Urith grey and strong with its square tower rising into the evening sky.

After a few minutes he turned and looked at the

villagers crowded onto the narrow pavement, some were pressed close to the hedge on the other side of which the sheep were lying down . He looked down the road at Aunty Pat's car with its hazards flashing, blocking the road. Aunty Pat was grinning and waving out of the window. Turning the other way he looked down the other end of the road towards the War memorial, a man and a woman with a hat on stood chatting in the middle of the road.

Everything and everyone was bathed in the dirty amber light cast by the street lights. What in God's name was he doing here, the Inspector asked himself. He felt like he was in a Simon Pegg movie. He had involved all of these innocent people in a very dangerous situation. So far no firearms had been used in the previous murders. He was counting on the fact that the killer wasn't armed, otherwise he'd lined up half the population of the village like a row of ducks ready to be wiped out in a matter of seconds.

And yet the killer without the assistance of firepower had still managed to kill three people. Whoever it was, was dangerous and willing to kill, for reasons he had yet to discover.

He knew he shouldn't have lost his temper with Ronald, the poor man was naturally anxious about his wife's safety, and it wasn't Ronald's fault that Celia had got involved. He would have to stop Ronald doing anything rash and deal with the man's natural impulse to dive in and save his wife. If he was honest with himself he felt quite out of his depth with the whole situation. Normally the murder team, senior officers, the hostage team along with helicopters and all manner of extras would have taken over.

At least he had been able to get the SOCOS in. He was just lucky that they had stopped down at Rosemoor for afternoon tea in the cafe on their way back from a training seminar. He must trust his instincts, there was only him, so he'd better get on with it. Trying to control his anxiety he tried to get things clear in his mind.

These murders must be connected in some way. The Colonel, the man in the churchyard, Mr Pope and now this hostage situation with the infuriating Mrs Ladygarden. Much as the woman was a thorn in his side, there was no way he could let another murder happen. Events had come full circle and now they had arrived back at the scene of the first murder, the Cottles cottage.

The inspector stared hard at the cottage as if he could bore a hole through the walls with his eyes. The murderer must be Dotty Cottle. Statistics showed, wives do kill their husbands. Mr Pope must have seen something and that's why she killed him. But why did she kill the man in the churchyard? He jumped as Billy touched his arm to attract his attention.

"Sorry sir but one of the SOCOs found this and thought you should see it straight away." He went to pass an evidence bag to the Inspector but he stopped him.

"Let me put some gloves on lad" The Inspector put his hands in his jacket pocket and felt for some latex gloves but pulled out his golfing gloves instead. It seemed an age ago that he'd come straight from the golf course. He put on the pair of latex gloves Billy had been given by the SOCO'S for him and took the bag and walked to the nearest street light. Inside was a passport and an ID card. Opening the bag he pulled out the passport, looked at it before putting it back and taking out the ID card.

"So we know from the passport that our mystery man

is Italian, I wonder what this ID is for?" He popped it back into the bag with the passport. "Well lad we'll give it to the experts when we get back, see what they can make of it."

"Sir, could Claire have a look at it, she might be able to translate it."

"Don't be stupid lad. We'll get it to the experts." Said the Inspector.

Billy couldn't quite keep the resentment out of his voice. "With respect sir that's going to take some time and Claire is fluent in French and Italian," he paused for effect "and Mandarin. Shall I fetch her?"

The Inspector flushed, knowing he shouldn't have made assumptions about the young PCSO muttered "Yes." Then gathering himself "thank you Billy."

Billy fetched Claire who after putting on gloves took the bag from the Inspector and took out the contents. After reading them she turned to the Inspector. "His name is Adriano Viti and he is a Vatican Tour Guide. I don't know what this means though, SNOTHP."

Surprised the Inspector mused "So our mystery man is from Rome and the Vatican no less. Now what on earth brought him to sleepy little St Urith? I thought he didn't look like a holiday maker, too formally dressed. This business is getting more confusing by the minute. Thank you Claire you've been very helpful. I wonder what those initials could mean"

Just then there was a high-pitched yapping coming from the Cottles and Hirsute Roley came hurtling through the gate and threw himself at Ronald.

"Now we've just got to get your mum out boy." He scooped him up and buried his face in the soft warm body for comfort and to hide his tears. He had been holding himself together pretty well until Hirsute Roley jumped into his arms. Once he gathered his composure he turned to the Inspector who was walking towards him.

"What are you planning on doing to get my wife out safely? It's getting to be a bit of a circus out here isn't it?" Ronald was doing his best to stay calm but he was worried that the Inspector was losing control of the situation and couldn't see a way forward.He would bet that the circumstances were out of the Inspector's experience but figured there must be a protocol for these situations. Since they had closed all the local police stations the chances of help coming in time were about as good as him winning a million on the premium bonds.

Just then several people turned their heads and looked up to the sky, including the Inspector.

Ronald hard of hearing hadn't heard anything but looked up anyway. Hirsute Roley started barking, then he saw the lights first then felt and heard the whoomph, whoomph of a helicopter.

"Bloody hell that's all I need, the police helicopter, a lot of good that is, I need men on the ground. The only thing that's likely to achieve is the suspect panicking." The inspector raged, clenching his fists at his sides, his complexion turning a fetching shade of puce.

Ronald decided he had better do something himself as the Inspector appeared to be losing his grip. Reaching down he clipped the lead onto Hirsute Roley's harness and walked a little way down the road till he was on his own and out of earshot. Pulling out his mobile phone he pressed menu and scrolled down to Celia's number.

32

THE MURDERER IS REVEALED

The atmosphere inside the Cottles cottage was very tense. The woman spoke to Nico and Dottie.

"I need to see what is going on out there. You two stay sat where you are, if you move she will pay the price."

She dragged Celia along with her as she left the kitchen and went into the sitting room. Crossing the room to the window, she pulled the curtain carefully aside.

"Kolos!" She grabbed Celia's arms and shook her roughly. " What did you say to your husband there are many people out there."

"You *heard* what I said, I didn't tell him anything."

Letting the curtain go she dragged Celia back into the kitchen. Looking directly at Nico she introduced herself.

"My name is Adrasteia."

Nico's expression stayed neutral for a moment and then his eyes widened in surprise.

"I see you remember me now Nico." The woman asserted.

"Adrasteia!" Nico expostulated "But what on earth are you doing here?"

"Nico, how do you know this woman?" Dotty had risen and was staring at Nico.

"Her family lives up the mountain next to the village I was brought up in, we went to the same school."

Dotty looking confused and scared asked "What does she want? What is she doing here? Are you in this together? I don't understand." She couldn't stop the tears.

Nico wanted to comfort Dotty and he struggled to pull his arms free, before giving up in frustration. "I don't know what she wants Dotty. Honestly. I haven't seen her in years. I don't know what she wants from us and there is definitely nothing between us."

"That's where you are wrong Nico, there is something very precious between us and our families and this is where it ends," Adrasteia said as she thrust Celia down onto a kitchen chair.

As Celia's bottom landed an enormous fart trapped by the cushion erupted through the front of her pyjama trousers. Even in such dire circumstances there was a bit of Dotty that wanted to giggle.

Luckily Andrea Bocelli burst forth from Celia's phone again, saving her further embarrassment. They all looked at it lying on the kitchen table before Adrasteia snapped. "Pick it up."

Celia picked it up.

"Who is it?" Adrasteia asked.

"I don't know. I can't see without my glasses and they're in my bag." Celia pointed to her bag hanging off of Nico's chair.

"You." She nodded at Dotty. "Pass that bag across and don't do anything silly."

Dotty who was sat next to Nico reached for the bag and unhooked it from the back of the chair, then slid it along the tabletop to Celia. By now the phone had stopped ringing but Celia found her glasses and she pressed on the screen until she found the caller information.

"It was Ronald." She said softly. "I'm not surprised he's tried to call me again, he must be very worried. I expect he's called in the Inspector. You know you might as well give up on whatever it is you are after. You have already killed three people, do you honestly think you can get away with killing three more?"

"You think I'm worried about a policeman, when I have all three of you? Nobody needs to get killed if these two co-operate. You get up" She pointed at Nico.

"Now both of you into the front room. I'll be right behind you with the old lady, so don't try anything."

"Will you stop calling me an old lady!" Celia was getting really cross, not so much about the knife digging into her neck, she had sort of got used to it but the old lady thing was really getting to her. She thought she looked pretty good for a woman of a certain age.

Adrasteia made Dotty and Nico sit on the floor under the window with their backs against the wall. From the darkened room, lit only by the borrowed light from the streetlamp, she looked out at the scene.

"Look at that mob out there, it's like a scene from an old Dracula movie, all they need is pitchforks to make it perfect. Now call your husband back and tell him I want to talk to him."

Suspicious, Celia asked. "Why do you want to speak to Ronald?"

"No you stupid woman, not your husband! The Inspector!"

"Oh." Celia found Ronald's number and pressed to connect. Although still scared, having an extremely sharp knife to your neck is not conducive to relaxation, she had spotted Hirsute Roley in Ronald's arms. The relief she felt buoyed her up. She was determined to take any chance she could so that they could all come out of this alive.

The woman Adrasteia, wanted something that was so important to her she was willing to kill for it and she obviously thought that Nico or Dotty had it. Whatever it was it couldn't be worth losing your life over and she was sure that she could persuade them to hand over whatever it was. "Hello Ronald?"

"Celia! Are you alright?" Ronald asked quite clearly distressed.

"Yes I'm fine Ronald don't worry I.."

"Shut up with the chat, tell him to pass you to the policeman." Adrasteia instructed as she dug the knife into Celia's neck.

Celia involuntarily gasped at the sharp pain and asked Ronald "Quick Ronald pass me to the Inspector."

"What's happening, are you being hurt?" Ronald was shouting down the phone.

Adrasteia grabbed the phone from Celia and snarled into the mobile "Yes she is and if you don't shut up and let me speak to the policeman, I will hurt her again."

"Oh, please don't hurt her, here is the Inspector." Ronald passed the phone over, whispering "It's a woman, she's holding Celia."

"Inspector Burke speaking, who is this?"

"That does not matter. Just listen, do as I say and nobody will get hurt."

"You have already murdered three people, you can't expect me to trust what you say?"

"You have no choice, I don't think you and a few country chickens peck pecking around in their cardigans can do anything to stop me. Now listen carefully and do exactly what I say. I shall be watching your every move. First get rid of the helicopter, then I want you to fetch my van a blue Citroen Berlingo. It's parked in the square with the keys under the mat, driver's side. I want it outside in the next five minutes. I want you park it and open the back doors, so I can see inside from back to front. Put the inside lights on so I can see there is no one inside. Then everyone and I mean everyone to move back down the road to the war memorial. I will be coming out with the old lady, so don't try anything. I will let her go when I am safely away." She threw the phone down onto the floor.

33
WHERE IS THE CURIOUS CURIOSITY?

Adrasteia looked at them and said "My van is ready and waiting, so let us now finish this Nico." She paused as she looked Nico and it was as if they were the only two people in the room.

"Many years ago my great great grandfather, a priest who lived in an isolated monastery was entrusted with the most sacred, holy, important and secret task a priest could ever be asked to do. He was probably chosen for this most special of tasks because he was obedient and unprepossessing in his darned and tattered habit. He certainly didn't look rich enough or important enough to be carrying anything anybody would want to steal.

His task was to collect a certain sacred object from it's resting place in a small church and take it all the way to the Vatican in Rome. There he was to place it in the hands of his Holiness the Pope.

On his journey he stopped for refreshments and a bed for the night at a taverna in a small village." Adrasteia paused "This is where his journey ended. That night the taverna owner stole the sacred object and a money bag that had been given for travel and food. My great great grandfather never made it to Rome and was excommunicated by the Roman Catholic Church. This was a permanent sorrow he carried till the end of his life and has remained a stain and a curse on my family for generations."

Dotty interrupted "That is a very sad story but what has it to do with any of us ?"

"Shut up! Nico, you don't look surprised. Is that because you know the story as well as I do?" Adrasteia asked him.

Celia had been listening fascinated, she loved a good story and suddenly all the pieces of the jigsaw were slotting into place. "Aah I see it all now."

"Really old woman, then why don't you tell us what you know, as Nico seems to have lost his tongue by the cat."

Celia asked "can I sit down only I'm feeling rather faint, I haven't eaten all day"

"I think you are plump enough to live off yourself for a few days. " Adrasteia commented as she backed up with Celia still in her grip to a small upholstered side chair and pulled it back to the window "Sit."

"Thank you" said Celia and proceeded to say what she thought. "Nico, I know that your family own a taverna and you told us just now that you lived near Adrasteia and went to the same school as her. So I'm confident in saying that it was one of your ancestors who stole the sacred item."

"My family aren't thieves, how dare you!" Nico shouted and tried to get up but was pushed back down by Adrasteia's foot.

"Stay where you are and shut up." Adrasteia nodded to Celia "Carry On."

"Dotty, you were married to the Colonel for some time. I'm surmising that you were not very happy in your marriage. I don't know what the circumstances were that caused this but possibly one of the factors could be that you spent long periods of time away from each other. It's also quite clear that you have been having a relationship with Nico for some time."

"I honestly didn't mean to start a relationship with anyone, especially as I was married. I was very unhappy in my marriage although the Colonel seemed quite content to jog along as we were. Fairly recently his behaviour became quite strange. One day when the Colonel was due to go away on his last tour of duty before retiring. I decided that I would do something for myself for a change instead of being bored and lonely, stuck in a house that I really didn't feel was mine. I went to Rhodes, somewhere I had never been before, the Colonel would certainly have never gone there for a holiday." She looked lovingly at Nico.

Celia continued "And that is where you met the handsome Nico." She wasn't averse to a handsome man.

"Yes." Smiled Dotty oblivious for the moment of the danger they were in as she looked at Nico.

Nico smiled back but then his face changed as he turned to look at Adrasteia. Then he turned from her and looked at Dotty, then Celia. "My mother fell down the stairs and died in broad daylight. She knew her way around our taverna even in the pitch dark of night, every doorway, every creaking board every step of the stairs. I do not believe it was an accident." He looked back at Adrasteia. "Did you kill my mother Adrasteia?"

"It was an accident. Your mother moved as quiet as a ghost. She was at the top of the stairs as I was coming out of her bedroom. I didn't mean for her to fall. It was her fault!" Adrasteia shouted.

"You evil heartless bitch!" Nico pushed down on his heels and tried to work his way up the wall with his hands.

"No you don't!" Adrasteia kicked him hard in the chest, the momentum caused the knife to nick Celia's neck.

"Shit that hurt! Stop Nico!" She shouted "I know you're angry but I'm going to get my throat cut here if you don't sit still. Now let's all calm down and I'll continue."

"You'd better get them to tell me where it is in the next five minutes old woman or I will have to start cutting his lover's fingers off." Adrasteia said quite chillingly calmly.

"OK, OK. Nico can I ask, is there something precious in your family that has been passed down from generation to generation?" Celia looked at Nico who went slightly red and replied.

"I can't believe you are accusing my family of being thieves, it's outrageous."

"There is no point in taking that attitude." Celia said firmly. "People are being murdered. Our lives are at stake. Nothing in this world can be worth letting people get killed over. Come on, quite clearly there's something you're hiding."

"Nico please tell Celia, for all our sakes." Dotty pleaded.

"Alright, yes there is a curiosity that my grandfather said must always be kept secret within the family . It protects us. I cannot believe that someone in my family stole it."

" Well I think we can all agree that Adrasteia's story sounds convincing. Your family live in the same village, own a taverna and have a secret curiosity that has been passed down the generations. I can only assume that the 'precious object' and the 'curiosity' are one and the same thing." Celia looked at Adrasteia. "Why do you think that the curiosity is here in the Cottles house?" Queried Celia.

"I followed these two to the airport and saw him pass it over, it was an easy matter to discover where she was flying to and who she was." Adrasteia boasted

"I realise I know now where the coloured dust came from that PCSO Boy found in the bathroom. It's the same reddish yellow colour as the earth at the recycling centre. I presume that you killed Colonel Cottle because he caught you looking for the curiosity."

"Phff he was a vain self-important man, easy to manipulate. I found the village where she lived" Adrasteia nodded at Dotty, "And watched them. With my experience It wasn't difficult to get a job nearby at the recycling centre. I could not believe my luck when I recognised her husband one day bringing in his garden waste, it was very easy to strike up a relationship."

"You had a relationship with my husband?" Burst out Dotty, surprised.

"Ha, so you are jealous now, what about your lover? Your husband he was a mataios, nothing happened. He enjoyed the flirtation but when I turned up at his house, he panicked, said his wife would be home any minute. When I said 'so what' he grabbed me roughly by both arms and started pushing me towards the side of the cottage saying I must go now but that he would meet me outside the recycling centre in an hour. So I left. But I came back."

"And you killed him." Said Celia "but why in such a strange way?"

"I thought I could get into the house while he was gardening but just to be safe I knock him out. That way I could search the house really fast and be gone by the time his wife came back."

"So what made you kill him?" Asked Celia, "Did he see you?"

"No, I crept up behind him and hit him with the end of the garden rake. When I looked down on him I could feel this great rage rise up in me. This man lived in luxury in his rich house and he had something that was taken from my family. I enjoyed the look on his face when he realised it was the end."

Dotty broke down and sobbed on Nico's shoulder.

"Huh you cry the alligator tears over your husband but you didn't want him, you wanted him!" Adrasteia indicated Nico.

"He was still my husband and I didn't want him dead." Sobbed Dottie.

Celia interrupted. "And you killed Pinky because he saw you I suppose?"

"Who is this Pinky, I did not kill any Pinky!"

"The man who lived next door."

"Phew silly little man. He sticks his head through the fence and asks if I'm a friend of the Colonels?'. I had to get rid of him."

"And I suppose you killed the occasional gentleman in the Churchyard because he was after the same thing?"

"You think you're so clever don't you but you don't know everything." Adrasteia spat.

"Then why don't you tell me?" Celia was buying as much time as she could, hoping that the police could find a way to rescue them. She was getting rather fed up with the knife digging into her neck. "And could you move that thing for a minute? I'm not going to do anything. As you say I'm an old woman." The last said through gritted teeth.

"Have you ever heard of SNOTHP?" Asked Adrasteia.

"Bless you." Said Celia.

"Very funny. You wouldn't think so if you ever met one of them. It stands for 'Sacred Ninja of the Holy Prepuce'. Does that mean anything to any of you?"

"No." Dotty and Nico said in unison.

"Well I know what the Holy Prepuce is but I have never heard of Snot whatever." Celia said with the hint of a smile.

"You may laugh but these people are highly trained killing machines only answerable to his holiness the Pope." Adrasteia said.

"If these people are highly trained killing machines, how did you manage to kill him?" Nico asked.

Adrasteia looked at Nico "Did you do your nine months national service conscription? I served three years in the Greek Army and I am trained to kill. I didn't know who he was when I killed him. It was a big mistake. I just thought it was some man trying to assault me."

"Why were you in the churchyard with this man?" Asked Celia.

"A note was left for me at the recycling centre, it said if I wanted the sacred object to be in the churchyard."

"I understand it all now. As I see it, there are two strands to this story. The first, is that the Vatican, acting for the Pope were trying to retrieve this lost relic. Adrasteia you also were trying to find it to return it to the Pope, thereby exonerating your family. If only you had known who that man was and where he had come from. You were both after the same thing. You could have let him find the Curiosity and return it. All of these deaths would have been avoided." Celia sighed.

"I really don't understand why the thing is so important that the Pope would want it. What is a Holy Prepuce?" Dotty asked in confusion.

"Well old woman, why don't you tell her, you think you know everything." Adrasteia mocked.

"I am seriously getting fed up with you calling me an old woman!" Celia snapped back.

Adrasteia pushed the tip of the knife into Celia's neck. "But you can't do anything about it can you?"

Celia waited a few moments and then started talking. " There are many stories and legends about Saints and religious relics. In fact there are still many relics in our churches here in England, although the churches don't like talking about them.. They purport to be pieces of a Saint's bone or scraps of their clothing.

Our own St Urith who the village was named after was a very young Brythonic maiden who had dedicated herself to God and a religious life. She was killed either by a rampaging haymaking gang of scythe wielding village maidens who were bribed by her wicked pagan stepmother. Or by a fleet of marauding Vikings. I think it is fair to say either could be true and we'll never know for certain. It is said that a fountain sprung up from the ground where her head fell and there is still a well here in the village to this day."

"Enough of your story telling, get to the point." Adrasteia interrupted.

Celia would have given her a dirty look if she'd been

able to turn her head but as the knife was still fairly close to her neck she didn't want to chance it.

"Some of the most famous and holiest of relics are associated with Jesus and in particular the Holy Prepuce. Jesus's foreskin. If I remember rightly there were hundreds of claims by various churches that they had the authentic Prepuce and it became embarrassing for the Catholic Church. So the Pope called for all of the Holy Prepuces to be brought to Rome. Nobody was allowed to write or speak about them again or they risked excommunication."

"I can't believe it. All this time we've had a piece of Jesus's di... foreskin, hidden in our cellar! That is so weird." Nico was astonished.

"So now we all know what it is, tell us where it is. Right now! Adrasteia shouted.

Nico turned to Dotty "Where is it Dotty?"

"It's in a packet of frozen peas in the freezer." She replied.

"For God's sake you stupid woman it had better not be damaged. Why did you put it in the freezer?" Adrasteia asked.

"I had to hide it from the Colonel and I knew he would never go in the freezer. Besides I didn't know what it was."

"It won't be damaged in any way. Freezing is a good way of preserving something." Nico tried to reassure Adrasteia.

"You!" Adrasteia looked at Dotty and threatened. " Fetch it and don't try anything silly or the old lady gets it."

"Unbelievable." Muttered Celia.

Dotty stood up slowly and walked out of the room heading for the kitchen. She did for one mad moment think about making a run for it through the front door but she wouldn't leave Nico.

The others in the front room could hear her rummaging about in the freezer, before she walked back into the room with a packet of frozen peas with a small bag laying on top "I don't want to touch it." She gave it to Adrasteia."Will you let us go now?" she asked hopefully.

"Sit back down and stay there both of you. Now you old woman get up slowly." Celia got up from the chair a little stiffly she had been sitting there for quite a while.

34

ADRASTEIA

Adrasteia whispered into Celia's ear. "Now listen to me, we are going to walk out of the door and when I say, we will walk down the path to my van. If you try anything I will slit your throat, I have killed before and you know I will do it again if I have to. I must and will return this to the Pope."

They walked to the front door like they were in some crazy three-legged race and Adrasteia looked through the peephole in the door before opening it. She pushed Celia forward and onto the path and stopped, listening and looking around but couldn't hear the helicopter or any other danger. She glanced down the path to where her van was parked. It was just outside the garden gate, it's inside light on showing that it was empty as instructed. She pushed Celia ahead of her slowly down the path, her head scanning from left to right.

Celia was as tense as the skin on a homemade rice pudding, she, like Adrasteia was looking around to see if help was on hand and if there was some way or something she could do to escape.

They reached the van and Adrasteia looked down the road towards the huddle of people looking back. She shouted to them "Everybody stay where they are or I'll kill the old woman!"

There were a few shouts of "bloody shame" and "don't worry Celia" and others unrepeatable but nobody moved.

Celia was waiting for her moment. She realised that Adrasteia was going to have to put her in the passenger seat first and then run around to the drivers side, this could be her one chance.

Adrasteia pushed Celia towards the driver's door. "Open it."

Celia stretched out her arm and opened the door.

"You're going to sit down and then slide over to the other side and don't try anything." Adrasteia threatened.

"Well really! That just about tops the lot. You don't seriously expect me to climb over the gearstick and the handbrake do you?" Celia protested as she sat down in the driver's seat.

"God you are the most infuriating woman I have ever met!" Adrasteia shouted as she drew back and put her hands on her hips."

Without the knife in her neck this was Celia's moment. With cries of "shit, shit, shit, shit, shit." She tried to kick out at Adrasteia but only managed to lift her leg about six inches. Changing tactics she punched her right fist into Adrasteia's stomach, reached out grabbed the door handle, pulling it shut and slammed her hand on the internal door lock.

Adrasteia screamed as she banged her fists on the window and kicked at the door "You bitch, open this door, I'll kill you." This was followed by a stream of unintelligible Greek. She was making so much noise she didn't hear PCSO Claire Pratt & PCSO Billy Boy running up behind her. She just felt her arms pulled back as she was slammed against the side of the van and a pair of handcuffs slapped on her wrists.

The Inspector who had puffed up behind them, pulled out his cotton hanky and picked up the knife.

Ronald tried to pull the van door open but it was still locked and Celia was sat rigid in the seat looking straight out of the windscreen.

"Celia let me in! Unlock the door." She didn't move. "It's me Ronald, open the door!" Celia didn't seem to hear him but pressed the button to unlock the doors. Ronald bent down to Celia and gently placed Hirsute Roley on her lap just as the passenger door opened.

"Hello dear, bet you're glad that nonsense is over. Fancy a cup of tea?" Aunty Pat dropped herself onto the passenger seat and closed the door at the same time as pulling out a small tartan thermos from her pocket. She unscrewed the cup, opened the flask and poured out the hot tea which definitely had a whiff of whisky about it, then lifted up Celia's hand placing the cup firmly in it.

Celia looked at the cup and automatically lifted it to her lips sipping the welcome comfort of hot tea before swallowing and coughing as the alcohol hit the back of her throat. She turned and smiled "aunty Pat, you are a lifesaver." Then she buried her face in Hirsute Roley's soft fur hiding the tears that she couldn't stop. Only looking up at the sound of cheering and people calling her name.

"Come on let's get you out." Ronald took Hirsute Roley and put him down then helped Celia out of the car.

Billy Boy moved close to the Inspector and thrust his Ipad in front of his face, "Look sir this is the evidence Celia told me to collect, this should help convict her sir.

This reddish/yellow dirt found on the Colonel's bathroom floor, that came from the dump and I've got the mower sir and.........."

"ENOUGH! P.C.S.O Boy. " The Inspector took Celia's hand and shook it. "Thank you Celia, go home now and if you feel up to it, can you come down to the station in the morning and make a statement."

"Will it be open and will there be any policeman in residence?" Asked Celia.

The inspector gave a wry smile and said. "Yes, I'll make sure of it. Shall we say 11 o'clock?"

"We'll see you then Inspector. Come on Celia quickly before everyone wants to ask you tons of questions." Ronald pulled Celia in the opposite direction of the advancing villagers.

"Dotty, Nico, come back with us and stay the night, we can travel into the police station tomorrow together. I don't know about you two but I could certainly do with something to eat and a large G & T."

"Well if you're sure Celia, I must admit I really don't fancy staying at home tonight." Answered Dottie.

Nico said. "That isn't your home any more. Your home is on Rhodes with me. Thank you Celia and Ronald."

They said their goodbyes to aunty Pat, Claire, Billy, Dusty, Betty and Harold and walked on towards home through the now quiet village. As they turned the corner into the alley they all jumped when a voice said.

"Ello my andsomes."

"God Willy, don't you think I've had enough shocks today?" Shouted Celia.

Willy chuckled and replied. "Nite nite my booty." He turned and walked off into the dark leaving 'odour de chicken' wafting in the air.

As Ronald closed the front door he turned to Celia. "I know we have to get through tomorrow but I hope after that we'll get back to normal. And please Celia, don't get mixed up in anything like this again will you."

"Of course not Ronald." She replied smiling as she went to fetch some glasses for the gin, her fingers crossed in front of her.

THE END

JUST IN CASE YOU ARE INTERESTED

St Urith was a Brythonic maiden. The Britons were an ancient Celtic people who lived in Britain from the Iron Age through the Roman and Sub-Roman periods. They spoke a language that is known as Common Brittonic.

Legend says that Saint Urith was born at East Stowford in Swimbridge Parish in North Devon, England. She was converted to Christianity and lived as a hermit in Chittlehampton, North Devon where she founded a church.

There are stories that say she was cut down either by:

A rampaging haymaking gang of scythe wielding village maidens who were bribed to kill her by her wicked pagan stepmother.

Or by a fleet of marauding Vikings. I think it is fair to say either could be true and we'll never know for certain. It is said that a fountain sprung up from the ground where her head fell and there is still a well there in the village to this day.

According to the Appledore History Society there are

ancient records of Northam written in the 10th/11th century containing a traditional story that says:

'Hubba the Dane' arrived with a fleet of 33 ships and marched to attack the Hill Fort at Kenwith. Legend states that they were defeated by Odun, Earl of Devon, he and 1000 of his men were killed. The men were buried at Bonehill and Odun in a cairn known as Hubbastone.

Today if you drive from Northam to Appledore in North Devon you will come across a Stone tablet at Bloody Corner, erected by Charles Chappell, which says:

Stop Stranger Stop,

Near this spot lies buried

King Hubba the Dane,

Who was slayed in a bloody retreat,

By King Alfred the Great.

There is also an area in 'The Copse', Northam Woods, which is called King Alfred's Cave and is reputed to be where King Alfred hid when being chased by the Vikings.

So it is possible Saint Urith was killed by an early Viking raid. Her feast day is the 8th July and Saint Urith's holy well still stands at the east end of Chittlehampton, North Devon, England.

With thanks to The Appledore History Society and Trinity College Library, Cambridge.

Why don't you come and visit North Devon, you won't be disappointed

Printed in Great Britain
by Amazon